Friendship
ADVENTURES

DreamWorks
PRESS

Los Angeles · New York

![DreamWorks]
STORYTELLERS
COLLECTION

Friendship
ADVENTURES

DreamWorks
PRESS

Los Angeles · New York

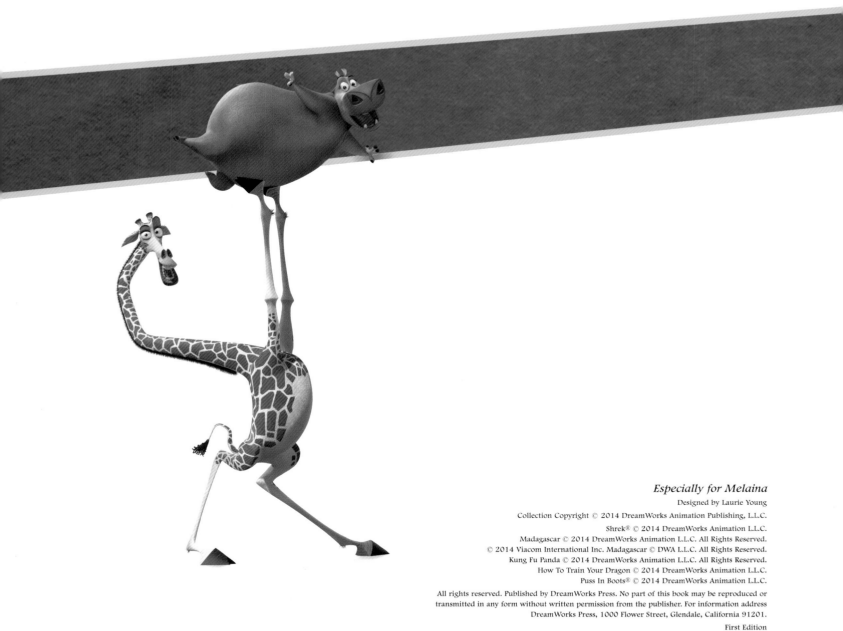

Especially for Melaina

Designed by Laurie Young

Collection Copyright © 2014 DreamWorks Animation Publishing, L.L.C.

Shrek® © 2014 DreamWorks Animation L.L.C.

Madagascar © 2014 DreamWorks Animation L.L.C. All Rights Reserved.
© 2014 Viacom International Inc. Madagascar © DWA L.L.C. All Rights Reserved.

Kung Fu Panda © 2014 DreamWorks Animation L.L.C. All Rights Reserved.

How To Train Your Dragon © 2014 DreamWorks Animation L.L.C.

Puss In Boots® © 2014 DreamWorks Animation L.L.C.

First Edition

Printed in China

1 2 3 4 5 6 7 8 9 10

08212014-A-1

ISBN 978-1-941341-00-1

Library of Congress Control Number: 2014939973

Visit dreamworkspress.com

TABLE OF CONTENTS

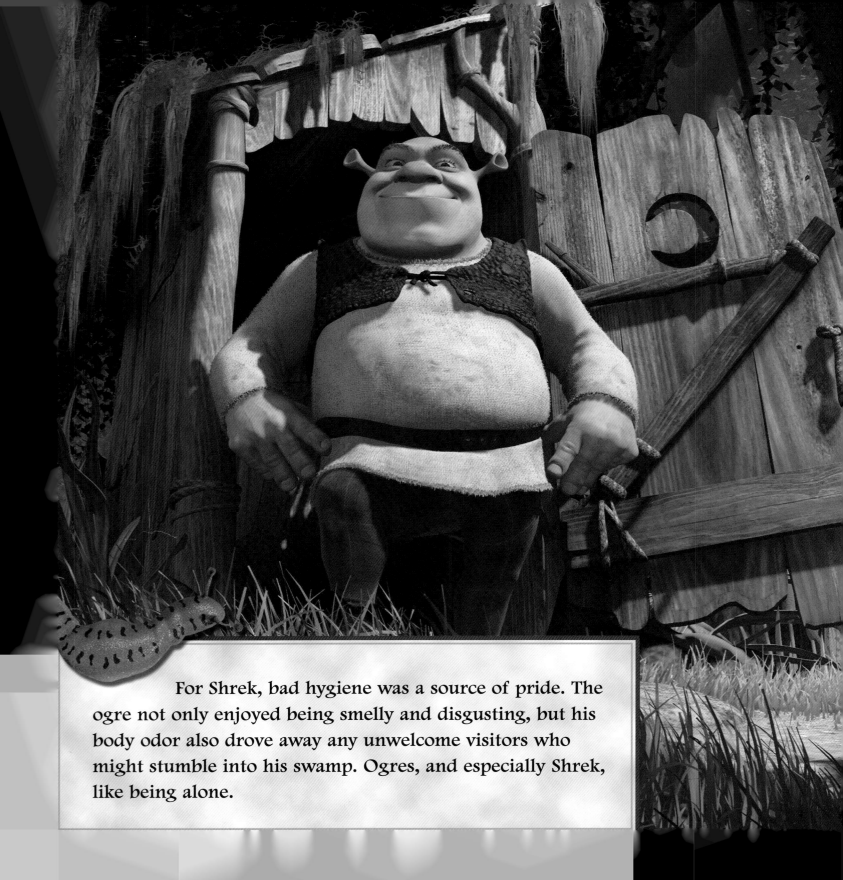

For Shrek, bad hygiene was a source of pride. The ogre not only enjoyed being smelly and disgusting, but his body odor also drove away any unwelcome visitors who might stumble into his swamp. Ogres, and especially Shrek, like being alone.

Shrek's Morning Routine

8:00 A.M.: Mud Shower

9:00 A.M.: Brush Teeth with Bug Guts

10:00 A.M.: Eyeball Breakfast

Of course, it took work to be so gross. Every morning, Shrek followed a strict messiness routine. In the afternoon, however, he could take a relaxing dip in his swamp. He waded into the murky waters, squatted comfortably, and then carbonated the swamp with a huge burst of gas that sent any living creature floating to the surface.

But Shrek's peaceful life was about to change. One evening, an angry mob of villagers from the neighboring land of DuLoc gathered on the edge of Shrek's swamp. They were hunting the ogre.

"All right, let's get it," said one villager.

"You can't just rush in there!" said another. "Do you have any idea what that thing will do to you?"

"Yeah," piped up a third villager. "It'll grind your bones for its bread."

"Actually, that would be a giant," said a helpful voice. The villagers turned to see who was correcting them. Standing behind them, his great green arms folded casually across his massive chest, was Shrek.

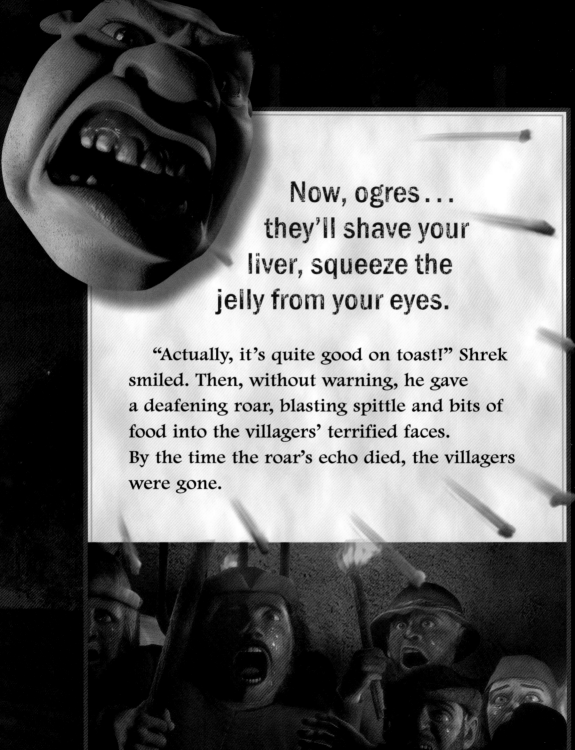

Now, ogres...
they'll shave your
liver, squeeze the
jelly from your eyes.

"Actually, it's quite good on toast!" Shrek smiled. Then, without warning, he gave a deafening roar, blasting spittle and bits of food into the villagers' terrified faces. By the time the roar's echo died, the villagers were gone.

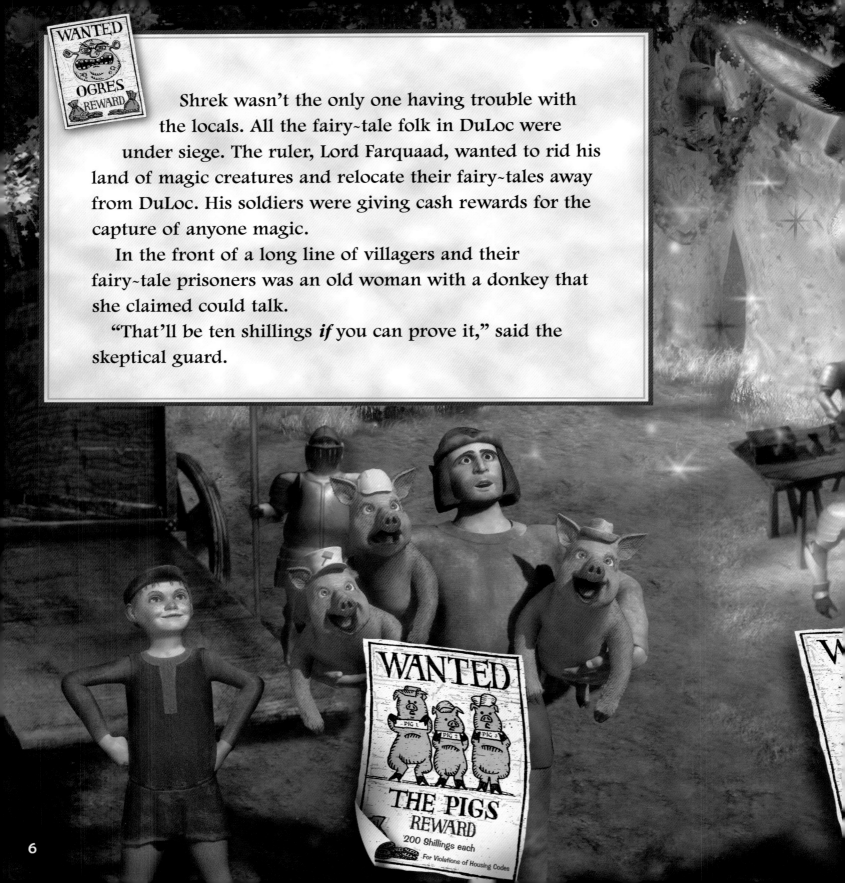

Shrek wasn't the only one having trouble with the locals. All the fairy-tale folk in DuLoc were under siege. The ruler, Lord Farquaad, wanted to rid his land of magic creatures and relocate their fairy-tales away from DuLoc. His soldiers were giving cash rewards for the capture of anyone magic.

In the front of a long line of villagers and their fairy-tale prisoners was an old woman with a donkey that she claimed could talk.

"That'll be ten shillings *if* you can prove it," said the skeptical guard.

WANTED

PINOCCHIO

Possessed Puppet whose nose has been
known to grow beyond the legal limit.
Claims he is a real boy.

REWARD

300 Shillings

WANTED
HUMPTY DUMPTY

REWARD

100 Shillings
Cracked-50 shillings
Sunny Side up-20 shillings
Scrambled-10 shillings

ANTED

IL FAIRIES
REWARD
25 Shillings

The donkey, who wasn't stupid, stayed silent. Farquaad's soldiers didn't have time for this nonsense, so they seized the old woman and dragged her away. But she had fight in her brittle bones, and as she struggled, her foot kicked a birdcage that held Tinkerbell. *Poof!* A cloud of fairy dust snowed down onto the donkey's hairy coat, and he slowly lifted off the ground like a balloon in the Thanksgiving Day Parade.

"I can fly!" Donkey exclaimed.

"He can talk!" said the guard.

"That's right, fool," said Donkey as he flew off toward the forest that bordered Shrek's swamp.

he fairy dust wore off, and Donkey hit the ground running. He galloped away from Farquaad's soldiers, going deep into the forest until he smacked into the smelliest tree trunk he had ever encountered. The tree trunk was Shrek's leg.

Now, few stay to chat with an ogre, so Shrek expected the donkey to scurry away in terror. The guards following him did. But Donkey was different. He not only wanted to come home with Shrek, he wanted to chat.

"I'll stick with you," he said. "Together we'll scare the spit out of anybody who crosses us."

This was too much friendliness for the ogre. He tried his favorite intimidation tactic: AAAARRRRR!!!!! But Donkey wasn't intimidated. He just kept on talking.

"Oh, Wow! That was really scary. And, if you don't mind me saying, if that don't work, your breath certainly will get the job done. 'Cuz you definitely need some *Tic Tacs* or something 'cuz your breath stinks! Man!"

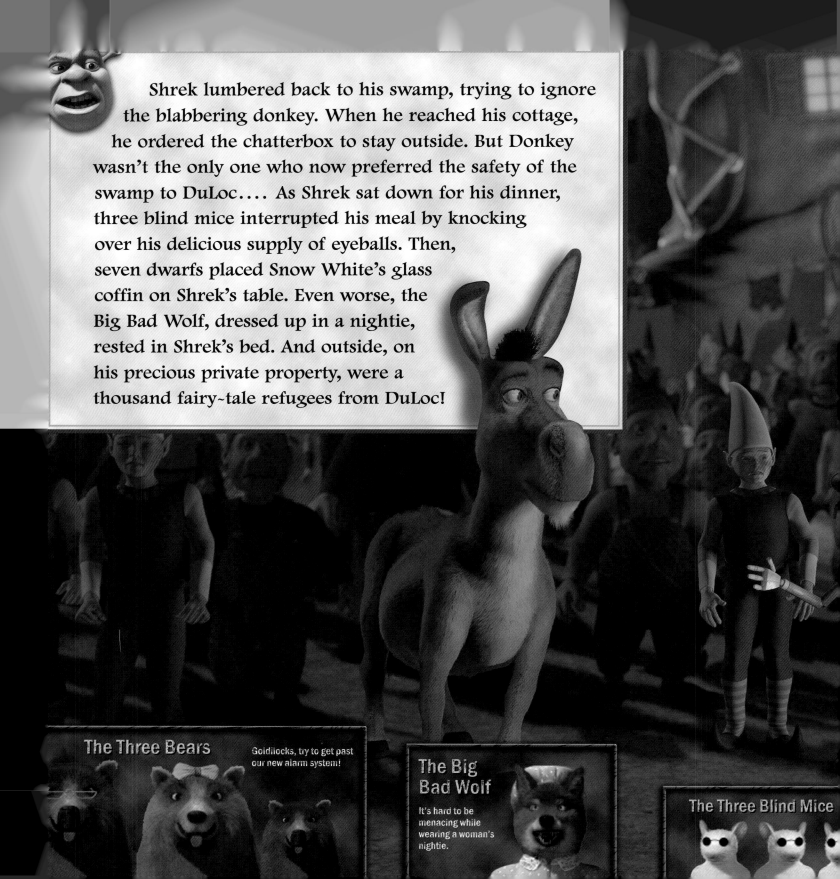

Shrek lumbered back to his swamp, trying to ignore the blabbering donkey. When he reached his cottage, he ordered the chatterbox to stay outside. But Donkey wasn't the only one who now preferred the safety of the swamp to DuLoc…. As Shrek sat down for his dinner, three blind mice interrupted his meal by knocking over his delicious supply of eyeballs. Then, seven dwarfs placed Snow White's glass coffin on Shrek's table. Even worse, the Big Bad Wolf, dressed up in a nightie, rested in Shrek's bed. And outside, on his precious private property, were a thousand fairy-tale refugees from DuLoc!

The Three Bears
Goldilocks, try to get past our new alarm system!

The Big Bad Wolf
It's hard to be menacing while wearing a woman's nightie.

The Three Blind Mice

"What are you doing in my swamp!!!" roared Shrek.

"We were forced to come here," said Pinocchio, his legs shaking with fear.

One of the three little pigs added, "Lord Farquaad! He huffed, and he puffed, and he—signed an eviction notice."

Shrek was used to being alone. So the presence of three visually impaired rodents, a comatose princess with her posse of seven dwarfs, and countless other folk made this not~so~jolly green giant pretty d*%& mad. Lord Farquaad was going to hear a roar or two from Shrek and if that didn't change his mind, then Donkey's endless chatter surely would!

Meanwhile, in DuLoc, Lord Farquaad's Master of Interrogation brutally dunked the Gingerbread Man into a glass of milk. Farquaad himself mercilessly plucked at the cookie man's gumdrop buttons.

"No! Not my gumdrop buttons!" pleaded the desperate cookie.

"Who's hiding the rest of the fairy-tale trash?" demanded Farquaad. He was a tiny man, yet enormously cruel and vain.

But the cookie wouldn't crumble. He was spared only by the arrival of a new victim, the Magic Mirror.

"Mirror, mirror, on the wall, is this not the most perfect kingdom of them all?" Lord Farquaad inquired.

The Magic Mirror reflected. "Well, technically, you're not a king," it said. Then the Magic Mirror showed Lord Farquaad three princesses and told him that by marrying one of them he would become a king, the King of DuLoc.

Farquaad chose Princess Fiona. But what about that dragon guarding her? His lordship wasn't going to break a nail fighting the beast. He'd find someone else to do it. He'd hold a tournament, and the champion would win the "honor" of rescuing the princess.

Bachelorette #1 is a mentally abused shut-in from a kingdom far, far away. Her hobbies include cooking and cleaning for her two evil stepsisters. Give it up for. . .

Cinderella.

Bachelorette #2 is a cape-wearing girl from the land of fancy. Just kiss her dead, frozen lips and find out what a live wire she is.

Please welcome. . .
Snow White.

Bachelorette #3 is a fiery redhead from a dragon-guarded castle surrounded by hot boiling lava. But don't let that cool you off. Yours for the rescuing. . .

Princess Fiona.

Welcome to DuLoc

farquaad's tournament began the day Shrek and Donkey arrived in DuLoc City.

AWFULLY PERFECT, the many signs claimed. Perfectly awful, thought Shrek. He was repulsed by the city's cleanliness.

There was no one in sight, so the pair began to search the eerie, artificial town for Lord Farquaad. They hadn't gotten far when they heard a trumpet blast.

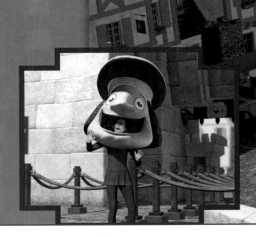

Greeter
Giant Farquaad head terrifies children and keeps them in line.

You are here.

Souvenirs
Along with popcorn and candy, you can buy Lord Farquaad dolls, shirts, pins, mugs, posters, knee pads, and books on his life.

Welcome Booth
Animatronic dolls spout musical propaganda:
Welcome to DuLoc. Such a perfect town.
Here we have some rules, let us lay them down.
Don't make waves, stay in line.
And we'll get along fine.
DuLoc is a perfect place.

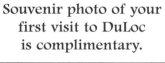

Souvenir photo of your first visit to DuLoc is complimentary.

Trams
Trams leave for "The Hassle at the Castle" at 1 P.M., 3 P.M., and 5 P.M. Watch knights sacrifice their lives for Lord Farquaad! No flash photography.

S

hrek and Donkey followed the sound into a stadium where Farquaad's knights were assembled in front of a sellout crowd. The orderly rows of contestants parted in terror as the giant green ogre stepped onto the field.

"Knights!" commanded Lord Farquaad. "New plan. The one who kills the ogre will be named champion."

The knights charged Shrek with swords drawn. His only choice was to fight.

The Donkey Punch:
The dirtiest move in the game. A swift kick that leaves a lucky horseshoe imprint for life.

The Ogre Vise:
Massive ogre hands apply pressure to the back of the opponent's skull; combination of restriction of blood flow to the brain and putrid stench from aired ogre armpits causes opponent to pass out.

Ye Olde Chair Shot

AIRPLANE SPIN

Tombstone
Pile
Driver

Lord Farquaad watched as the surprisingly nimble Shrek knocked down each knight with moves worthy of a professional wrestler. Even Donkey took down a man or two.

"Congratulations, Ogre," Farquaad said as if he had planned this outcome. "You've won the honor of embarking on a great quest."

"I'm already on a quest," replied Shrek. "A quest to get my swamp back."

"All right, Ogre, I'll make you a deal," said the wily lord. "Rescue Princess Fiona for me, and I'll give you your swamp back."

Shrek had to agree.

17

"I don't get it, Shrek," said Donkey as the pair left DuLoc. "Why didn't you pull some of that ogre stuff? You know, grind his bones to make your bread."

"For *your* information," answered Shrek, "there's a lot more to ogres than people think. Ogres are like"— Shrek glanced down at an onion he was snacking on—"onions. They both have layers."

Donkey thought for a moment. "You know, not everybody likes onions," he said helpfully. "Cake! Everybody likes cake! Cakes have layers."

Donkey, though he meant well, had missed Shrek's point. No one understood that ogres, like everybody else, are complicated. They aren't just big ugly monsters. They have feelings and dreams underneath their scary exterior.

SHREK, I'M LOOKING DOWN!

Before long, the flowery fields of DuLoc gave way to a barren wasteland of dark jagged rocks. A pungent odor filled the air.

"Whew, Shrek!" gasped Donkey. "Did you do that? You gotta warn somebody before you crack one off!"

"Believe me," Shrek snapped back, "if it was me, you'd be dead." He sniffed the air. "It's brimstone. We must be getting close to the Dragon's Keep."

And there it was: a burned and blackened castle perched on a rocky pinnacle over a lake of molten lava. A single rickety bridge stretched over the boiling moat. Shrek walked onto the bridge, feeling it sag under his great weight but Donkey froze.

"We'll tackle this together," assured Shrek. **"Just don't look down."**

"I'll handle the dragon. You go over
there and find some stairs," ordered
Shrek as they entered the dark,
cavernous keep. "The princess will be
up the stairs, in the tallest tower."

"What makes you think she'll be
there?" Donkey asked, surprised
by the ogre's sudden expertise in
princesses.

"I read it in a book once,"
said Shrek.

Donkey was glad he didn't have
to look for the dragon. Stairs were
scary enough for him. Unfortunately,
ten steps down the dark corridor,
Donkey found himself eyeball~to~
eyeball with—a massive red
dragon! He turned and fled,
chased by a fireball of dragon breath.
Shrek quickly shoved Donkey out of
the fireball's blazing path. Donkey
just kept running, with the dragon
in pursuit.

"Gotcha!"

ONCE UPON A TIME THERE WAS A LOVELY PRINCESS

SHE WAS locked away IN A CASTLE GUARDED BY A TERRIBLE FIRE BREATHING DRAGON

MANY BRAVE KNIGHTS had attempted to FREE HER FROM THIS DREADFUL PRISON

BUT NONE PREVAILED

SHE WAITED IN THE DRAGONS KEEP. IN THE HIGHEST ROOM OF THE TALLEST TOWER

FOR HER TRUE LOVE AND TRUE LOVE'S FIRST KISS

Shrek shouted as he grabbed the beast's tail. But the dragon, with an easy flick, sent the ogre flying high into the air and right through the roof of the tallest tower.

Now the dragon could focus on poor Donkey.

Shrek crash-landed in Princess Fiona's bedchamber. There she lay peacefully asleep. Why do princesses seem to sleep so much? wondered Shrek. The Princess and the Pea, Snow White, Sleeping Beauty: all a bunch of royal sleepyheads.

"Are you Princess Fiona?" asked Shrek, attempting to wake her with a forceful shake.

"I am," she said as if she had rehearsed this line many times. "Awaiting a knight as bold as you to rescue me."

"Let's go," he said abruptly.

"But wait," pleaded Fiona. "This be-eth our first meeting. Should it not be a wonderful, romantic moment?" It was clear the princess thought the armor-clad ogre was her handsome prince.

"No time." Shrek grabbed Fiona by the arm and hauled her away as the dragon roared below. He had to rescue Donkey.

Dear Diary,

Slept late again. Looked out the window and pined for Prince. (Note: Getting really good at pining.) Did a nice cover version of "Someday My Prince Will Come" with more of an R & B sound. But it kept being interrupted by the screams of unfortunate adventurers who had stumbled upon the dragon. Being locked in a tower 24-7 can make a girl crazy. Woe is me. Woe is I, I should say (a princess can never be too precise with her grammar!). I am beginning to think my prince may never come, and I'll grow old alone in this tower.

Mrs. Prince Charming

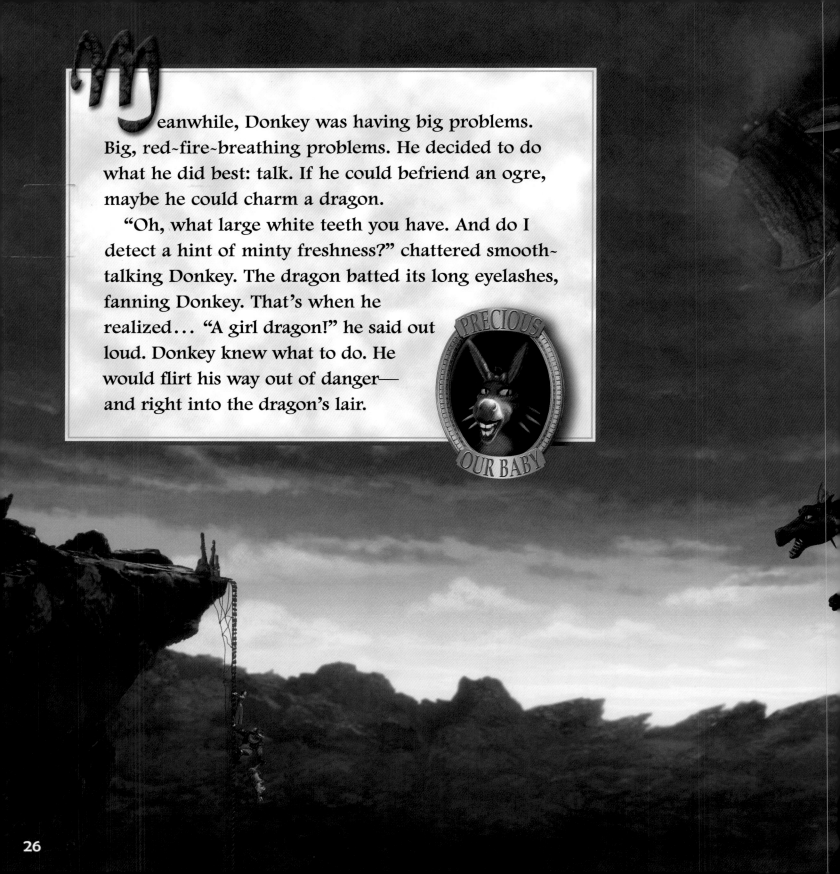

eanwhile, Donkey was having big problems.
Big, red-fire-breathing problems. He decided to do
what he did best: talk. If he could befriend an ogre,
maybe he could charm a dragon.

"Oh, what large white teeth you have. And do I
detect a hint of minty freshness?" chattered smooth-
talking Donkey. The dragon batted its long eyelashes,
fanning Donkey. That's when he
realized... "A girl dragon!" he said out
loud. Donkey knew what to do. He
would flirt his way out of danger—
and right into the dragon's lair.

PRECIOUS

OUR BABY

Dragon clutched him in her coiled
tail and breathed heart~shaped smoke
rings in his startled face.

Just as the dragon pursed her lips
and went in for a kiss, Shrek swung
down on a candelabra chain and tried
to grab Donkey. *THWUMP!* Shrek
missed and instead received Dragon's
wet one on his butt. He let go of the
chain, and as it went up, the candelabra
came down, landing like a collar around
the dragon's neck. Shrek, Donkey, and
Fiona made a run for it, with Dragon
stuck like a dog on a leash.

"You did it! You rescued me!" Fiona cheered after they made it back over the bridge and onto safe ground. Her fairy-tale was coming true, after all.

Now it was time for the long-expected kiss, the one she had waited for all those years. The one she had practiced on her pillow so often. In her most imperious voice, the princess demanded that the knight take off his helmet. When at last he did so, Fiona just stared at him blankly. "You're… an ogre?" she asked, though it was obvious.

Shrek explained the situation to the disappointed princess, "I was sent to rescue you by Lord Farquaad. He's the one who wants to marry you."

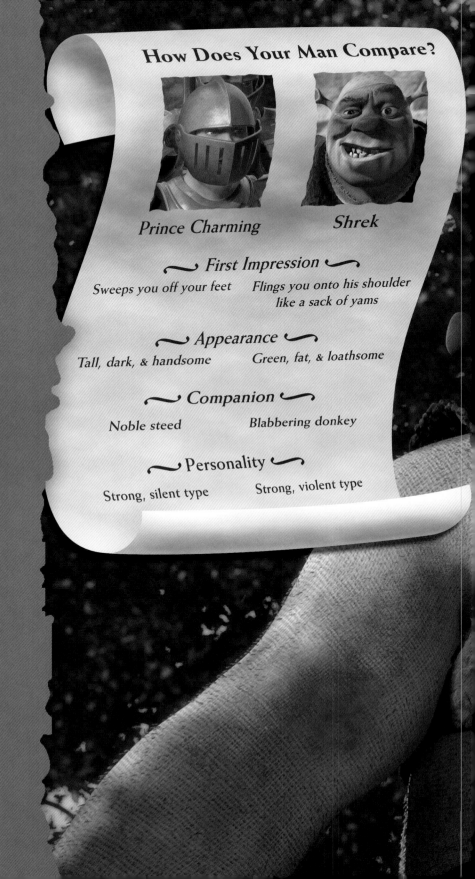

How Does Your Man Compare?

Prince Charming   Shrek

First Impression

Sweeps you off your feet   Flings you onto his shoulder like a sack of yams

Appearance

Tall, dark, & handsome   Green, fat, & loathsome

Companion

Noble steed   Blabbering donkey

Personality

Strong, silent type   Strong, violent type

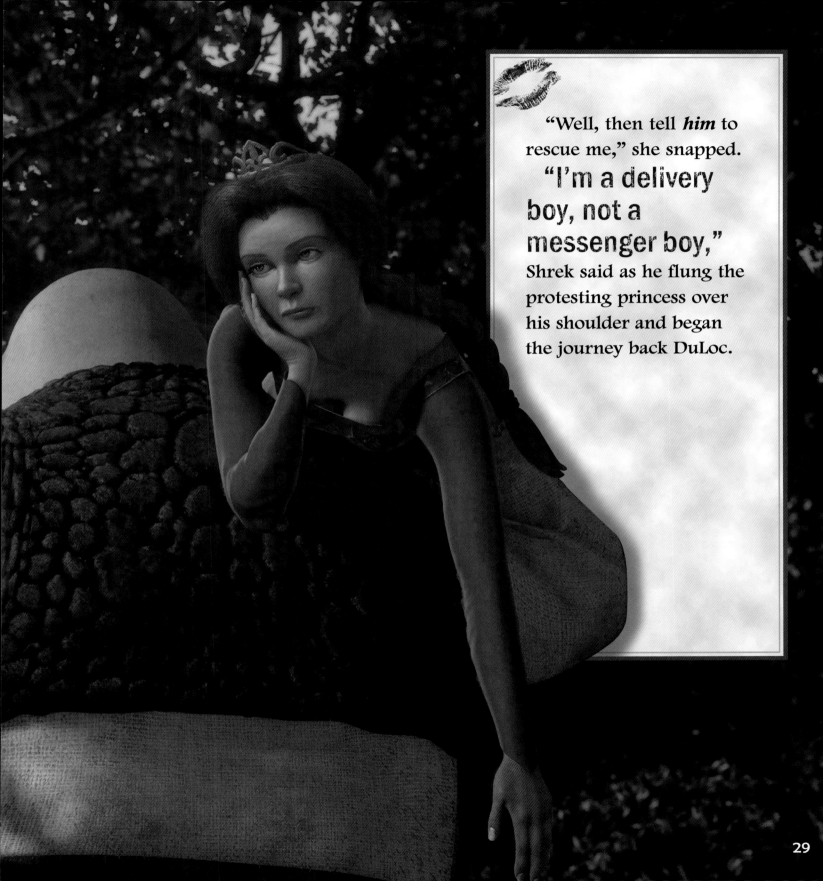

"Well, then tell *him* to rescue me," she snapped. "I'm a delivery boy, not a messenger boy," Shrek said as he flung the protesting princess over his shoulder and began the journey back DuLoc.

29

Shrek, carrying Fiona over his shoulder, walked steadily for the rest of the day, determined to deliver Farquaad's bride as soon as possible.

Fiona had finally stopped fuming and was now chatting with Donkey. As the sun began to set, she suddenly asked, "Shouldn't we stop to make camp?"

Shrek ignored her until he was interrupted by a voice that seemed too loud and large for a princess: "I need to find somewhere to camp now!"

So they camped. Fiona, demanding privacy, hid herself in a nearby cave just as the sun disappeared. Shrek and Donkey lay outside, gazing at a night sky full of stars.

Bloodnut the Flatulent
This ogre could knock men out with his potent stench

Gerald the Pear-Shaped

An ogre who once ate 4,000 live fish to lower the level of a river and keep it from flooding an ogre village

Throwback

The only ogre to ever spit over three wheat fields

"There's Bloodnut the Flatulent," Shrek explained, pointing to a constellation.

Donkey couldn't see the shape. "Man, it ain't nothing but a bunch of little dots."

Shrek was a little irritated. "Sometimes things are more than they appear," he said, thinking more about himself than the stars. Donkey may not have understood Shrek, but Fiona, listening from her cave, nodded in sympathy.

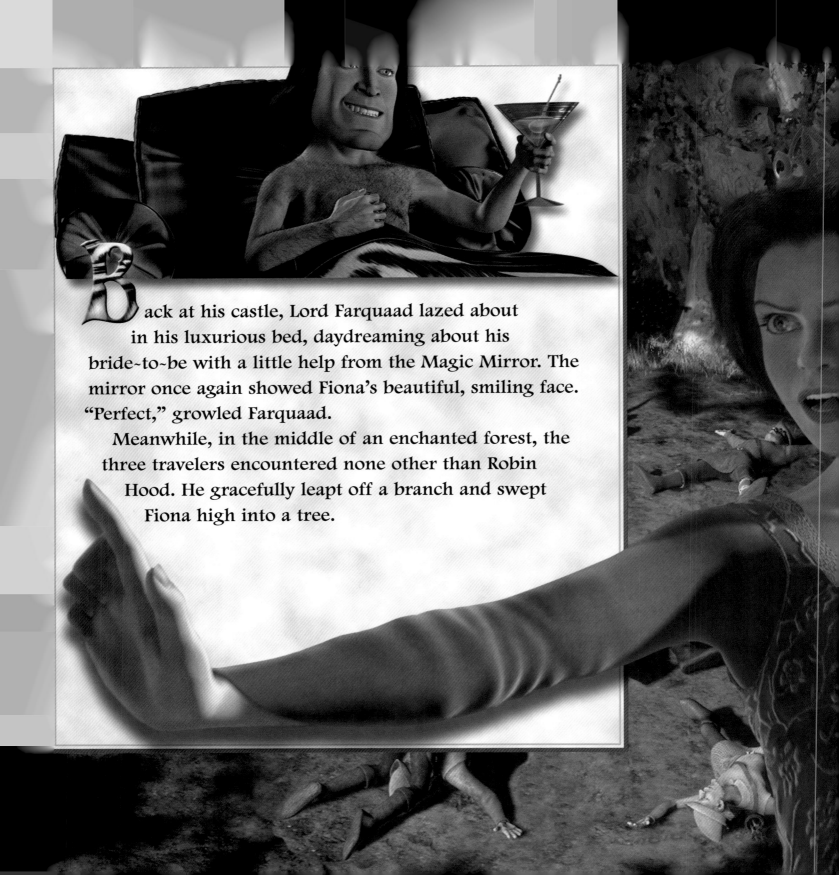

ack at his castle, Lord Farquaad lazed about
in his luxurious bed, daydreaming about his
bride-to-be with a little help from the Magic Mirror. The
mirror once again showed Fiona's beautiful, smiling face.
"Perfect," growled Farquaad.

Meanwhile, in the middle of an enchanted forest, the
three travelers encountered none other than Robin
Hood. He gracefully leapt off a branch and swept
Fiona high into a tree.

"I am your savior and I am rescuing you from this green beast," Hood said smoothly. He then jumped to the ground, drew his sword, and called out, "Oh, Merry Men!"

Shrek was outnumbered. But before the Merry Men could attack, Fiona swung into karate action.

"Hiyaaaah!" she cried. Within minutes, she had knocked out Robin and every Merry Man with a series of skillful backhands, flying kicks, and expert punches.

When she finished, Fiona simply smoothed out her dress, smiled, and continued on her way with Shrek and Donkey following in stunned silence.

OOOWWW!

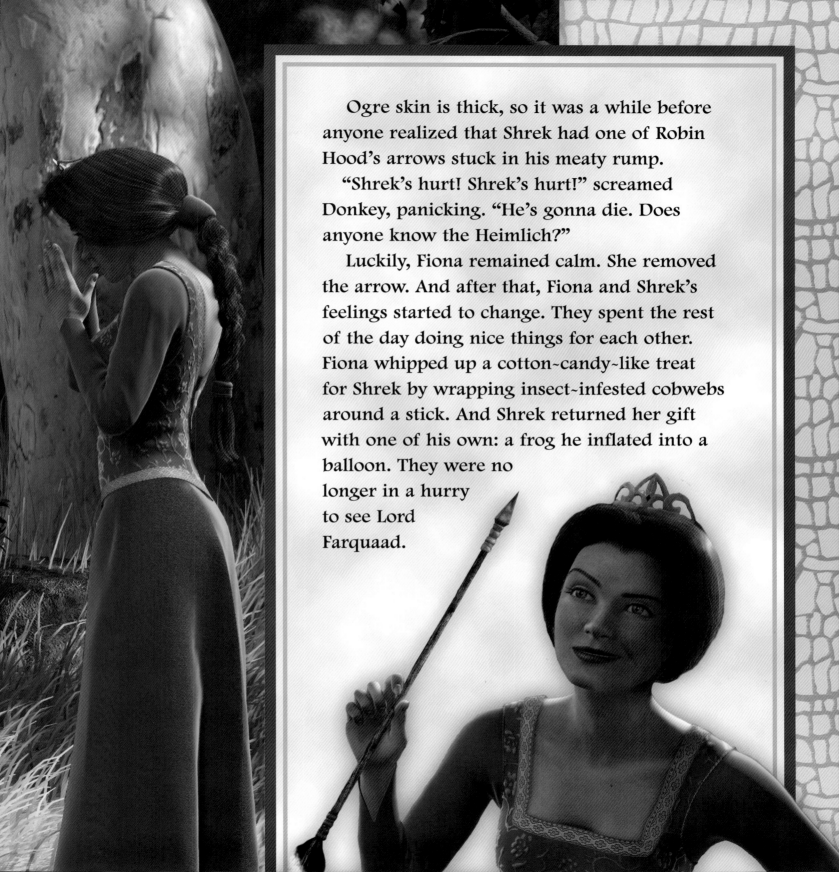

Ogre skin is thick, so it was a while before anyone realized that Shrek had one of Robin Hood's arrows stuck in his meaty rump.

"Shrek's hurt! Shrek's hurt!" screamed Donkey, panicking. "He's gonna die. Does anyone know the Heimlich?"

Luckily, Fiona remained calm. She removed the arrow. And after that, Fiona and Shrek's feelings started to change. They spent the rest of the day doing nice things for each other. Fiona whipped up a cotton-candy-like treat for Shrek by wrapping insect-infested cobwebs around a stick. And Shrek returned her gift with one of his own: a frog he inflated into a balloon. They were no longer in a hurry to see Lord Farquaad.

They made camp that afternoon by an old mill outside DuLoc City. Shrek cooked up one of his specialties: weedrat, rotisserie style.

"This is delicious," said Fiona, wolfing down the rat with an appetite not fit for a princess.

Owl-Brain Ball

Sprinkle owl brains with bloodworms. Place contents in mouth. Chew for 2 to 3 minutes. Remove from mouth. Let bake in sun for 5 days. Juggle. Eat.

Stuffed Possum Pops (on a stick)

Find 4 roadkilled possums. Stuff possum cavities with 2 teaspoons maggots, 1 ounce bird beaks, 2 tablespoons fish eyes, and loose change. Marinate in swamp for 2 hours. Shove tree branch into possum. Ready to serve.

Ant Sock

Grab handful of ants.
Put in sock.
Eat.

As the princess and ogre gazed at each other, Donkey interrupted. "Man, isn't this romantic? Just look at that sunset," he said, oblivious to the look being shared by his two companions. That was Fiona's cue. With a quick *good-night*, she raced into the mill.

Donkey took a long look at Shrek. "I see what's going on," he said. "I'm an animal, and I got instincts. I know you two were digging each other. Just go in and tell her how you feel."

"There's nothing to tell," said Shrek. "She's a princess and I'm an ogre."

Donkey decided to play matchmaker. He crept into the mill to talk to the princess, but the figure he saw in the shadows wasn't Fiona. It was an ogress! Donkey screamed.

"Shhhhh! It's me. The princess!" hushed the ogress. "In this body!"

"Oh no! You ate the princess!" cried Donkey in horror.

"No," she explained. "When I was a little girl, a witch cast a spell on me. Every night I become this horrible ugly beast. That's why I have to marry Lord Farquaad tomorrow before the sun sets and he sees me like this. Only true love's first kiss can break the spell," she finished with a sob.

VOGRE|MAGAZINE

Beauty Tips for Ogresses

1 Grind fish scales for shimmery eye shadow

2 Exfoliate weekly with armadillo paw

3 Use swamp mud as face mask

Ogression PERFUME

Donkey had calmed down now. "What if you don't marry Lord Farquaad?" he suggested. "What if you married Shrek?"

"Take a good look at me, Donkey," she said.

At that moment, Shrek had approached the mill door, holding a flower he'd picked for Fiona. He had decided to tell her how he felt, but he froze when he heard the princess speak,

"Who could ever love a beast so hideous and ugly?"

Shrek thought she was talking about him, and both his heart and flower wilted at her words.

The next morning, Princess Fiona walked out of the old mill and saw Shrek stomping toward her.

"I've bought you a little something," he sneered. The little something was Lord Farquaad and his army.

Shrek took one last angry look at Fiona, snatched the deed to his swamp from Farquaad's hand, and stormed off.

FROM THE DESK OF
Lord
Farquaad

Perfect
Wedding Planner

☑ On wedding cake, put extra icing under groom to make him look taller.

☑ Use Gingerbread Man for cake crust.

☑ Steal golden ring from lazy partridge in pear tree.

☑ Take Tom Thumb's platform shoes.

The pint-size Prince Charming approached his beautiful bride-to-be. "Princess," Lord Farquaad said, after looking her over like a new car, "will you be the perfect bride for the perfect groom?"

Fiona shot an angry glance at Shrek's distant form. "Let's get married today."

Farquaad readily agreed. He and Fiona rode off together, and Donkey, with an anxious last look at Fiona, hurried after Shrek.

Safety Card for Dragon Airlines

Remain seated at all times. In the event of a crash, the person next to you may be used as a flotation device.

Exits are located all around you. In an emergency landing, flee, screaming like a baby, onto the wing until the dragon lands. In case of fire (and there will definitely be fire), stay on the dragon's good side.

If experiencing motion discomfort, lean over the side of the dragon and let loose. Because of wind resistance, don't face forward!

Back in his swamp, Shrek sat down for some fried weedrat in gerblecky. But, for the first time ever, he had no appetite. Suddenly, he heard a noise outside. It was Donkey.

"Back off," warned Shrek. He wasn't in the mood to see anyone.

But Donkey stood his ground. "You're so wrapped up in layers, onion boy, you're afraid of your own feelings. Just like with Fiona. All she ever did was like you. Maybe even love you."

That got Shrek's attention. "Love me? She said I was ugly! A hideous creature. I heard you talking."

"She wasn't talking about you! She..." Donkey stopped. He had promised to keep the princess's secret, but he'd said enough. Shrek knew he had to stop the wedding.

"We'll never make it in time," he groaned.

Donkey whistled and Dragon appeared, hovering overhead like a rescue helicopter.

"I guess it's just my animal magnetism," said Donkey with a wink.

By night one way, by day another.
Until you find true love's first kiss.
And then take love's true form.

44

s Dragon soared toward DuLoc City, the wedding ceremony had already begun.

Fiona glanced nervously at the window, where the sun was dropping toward the horizon. "Could we just skip ahead to the end?" she asked.

The priest complied and made it official. There was only one thing left to do: Farquaad stood on his tiptoes to kiss Fiona.

Just then, Shrek burst through the cathedral doors. **"I object!"** he roared. "You can't marry him, Fiona. He's just marrying you to be king." He charged to the altar.

"He's not your true love," said Shrek, looking deeply into Fiona's eyes.

Lord Farquaad laughed. "This is precious! The ogre has fallen in love with the princess."

"Is this true?" Fiona stepped forward.

At that moment, the sun set. A sudden burst of light and clouds of smoke shrouded Fiona. She began to transform. When the smoke finally cleared, a plump green ogress stood in her place. Farquaad's eyes grew wide with revulsion. The wedding guests gasped in horror.

"Well, that explains a lot," said Shrek.

"This marriage is binding!" cried Farquaad. "I am still king." He placed the royal crown on top of his head. "And as king, I order you knights to kill the ogre. And you, Princess..." Farquaad grabbed the ogress. "I'll have you locked up in that tower for the rest of your life."

Farquaad's men surrounded Shrek. He knocked several to the ground before they managed to hold him. Still struggling, he gave a piercing whistle and Dragon came crashing through the window behind the altar. She swallowed Lord Farquaad in one great gulp.

"Nobody move," threatened Donkey from his seat on her head. **"I've got a dragon and I'm not afraid to use it."**

Dragon belched and out rolled Farquaad's crown.

Shrek turned to Fiona. "Fiona," he said—this time he wasn't going to chicken out—"I love you."

"I love you, too," Fiona said.

Fiona and Shrek kissed. Then the ogress began to lift into the air and was once again shrouded in flashing light. Finally, Fiona fell to the floor. The crowd waited in suspense to discover what love's true form would be. When Fiona rose again... she was still an ogress.

She felt her face. "I don't understand. I'm supposed to be beautiful."

"But you are beautiful," said Shrek.

gre and ogress joined hands in smelly matrimony as DuLocians and fairy-tale creatures watched happily. Fiona hurled her bridal bouquet into the crowd where Sleeping Beauty and Snow White battled over the prize. But sly Dragon quickly snatched the flowers in her snout, glancing at Donkey with a smile.

With a wave of her wand, a fairy godmother transformed a wild onion into a majestic carriage. The newlyweds hopped into their layered coach, waving to the crowd as they rode off into the sunset.

And they lived together, ugly ever after.

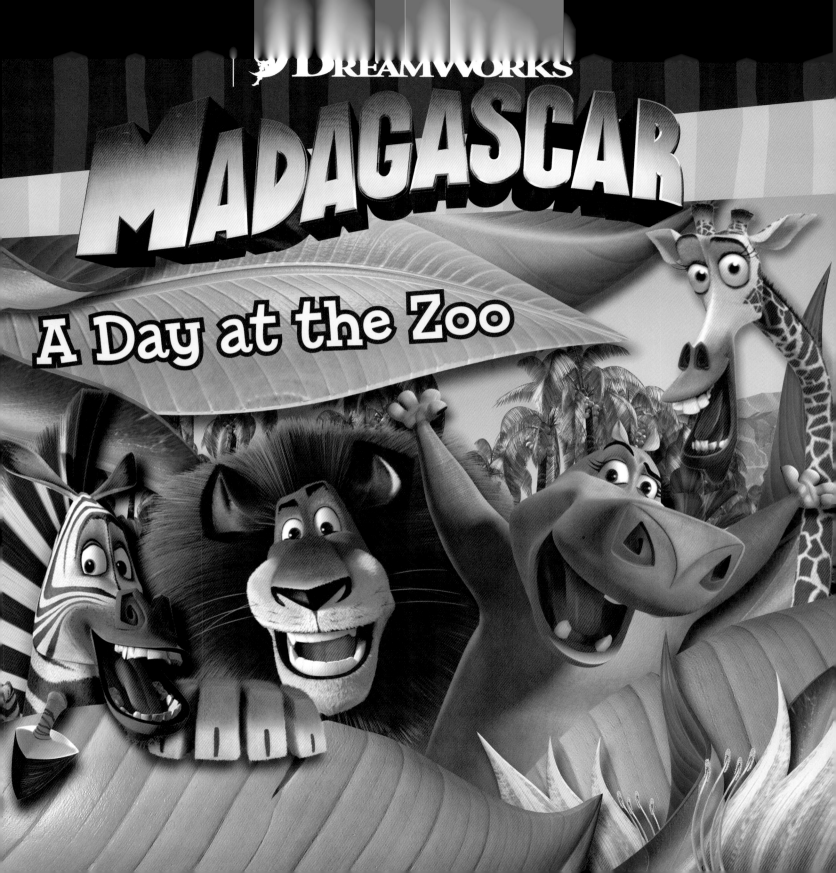

People began to pour through the zoo gates, hurrying to see their favorite animals.

The star of the show, Alex the lion, climbed onto a fake rock and struck a majestic pose.

"It's showtime!" Marty the zebra said. He moonwalked and made armpit noises. Now for the big finish! He took a mouthful of water and sprayed the crowd like a fire hose. The children loved it, but the adults weren't so thrilled.

After the crowd had left, Marty was bored. And a little let down. Was anything exciting ever going to happen? Suddenly four penguins popped up in his pen. They were holding spoons, which they were using to dig a tunnel.

"What continent is this?" asked Skipper, the penguins' leader.

"Manhattan," Marty said.

"We're still in New York! Abort! Dive! Dive! Dive!" cried Skipper, and all the penguins disappeared back down the hole.

"Wait!" Marty cried. "What are you guys doing?"

"We're going to the wide-open spaces of Antarctica. To the wild!" Skipper said, sticking his head back out of the hole.

"The wild? You can actually go there?" Marty asked.

But the penguins were gone.

That night, Alex, Gloria the hippo, and Melman the giraffe had a birthday party for Marty. There were presents and a cake.

"Make a wish," said Gloria. Marty thought for a few seconds, then blew out the candles.

"C'mon, what'd ya wish for?" Alex asked.

"I wished I could go to the wild!" Marty announced.

"But it's unsanitary!" said Melman. He hated germs.

"Doesn't it bother you that you don't know anything about life outside this zoo?" Marty asked.

"Nope," was the unanimous reply.

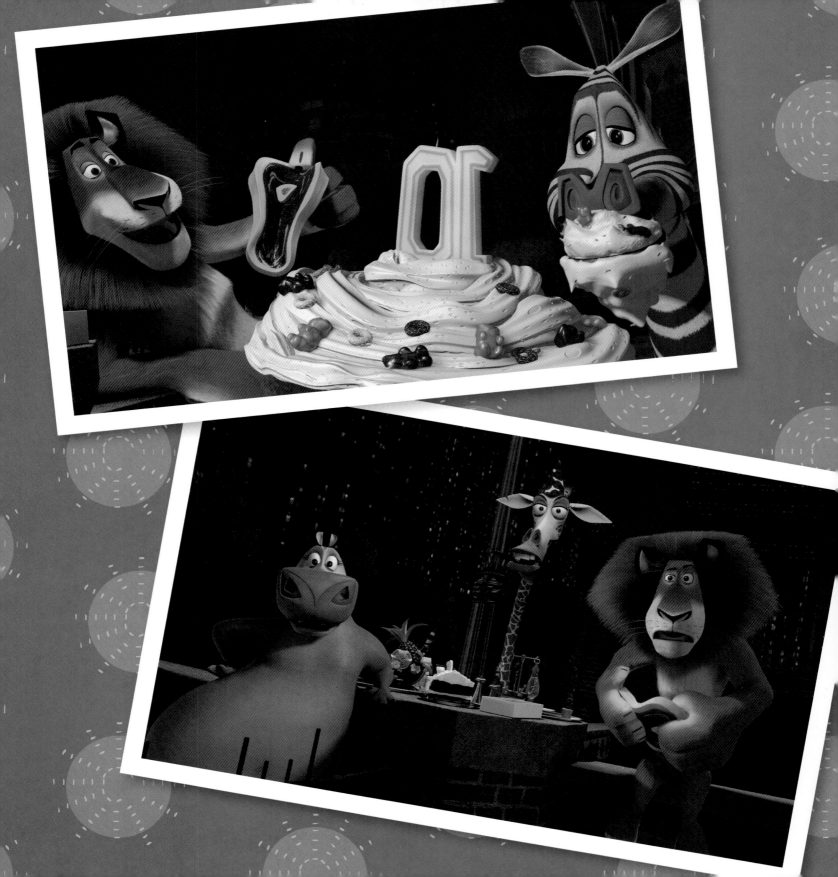

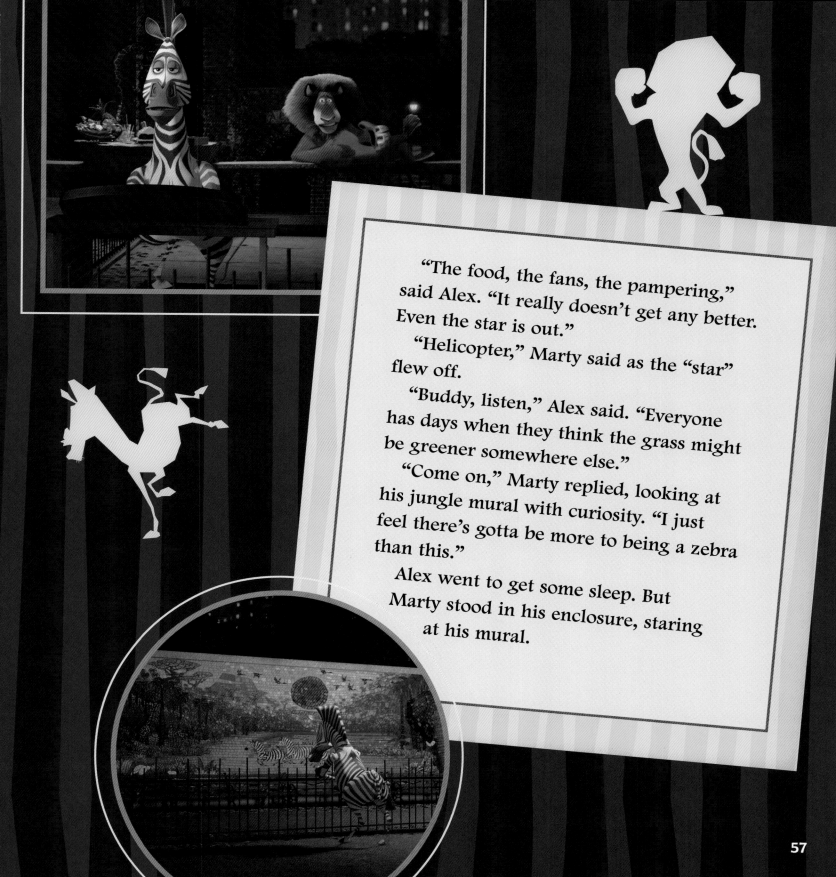

"The food, the fans, the pampering," said Alex. "It really doesn't get any better. Even the star is out."

"Helicopter," Marty said as the "star" flew off.

"Buddy, listen," Alex said. "Everyone has days when they think the grass might be greener somewhere else."

"Come on," Marty replied, looking at his jungle mural with curiosity. "I just feel there's gotta be more to being a zebra than this."

Alex went to get some sleep. But Marty stood in his enclosure, staring at his mural.

58

"Alex. Alex! It's Marty!" Melman cried. "He's gone."

"Where would he go?" asked Gloria.

"The wild," Alex replied. "If the people find out, they're going to be mad. We gotta go after him."

Now the three friends were really worried. They had to find Marty. They decided to go to the train station to look for him.

Meanwhile, Marty was enjoying all that Manhattan had to offer—strutting the streets, talking to a police horse in Times Square, even ice-skating! At last, he was on his way to the wild.

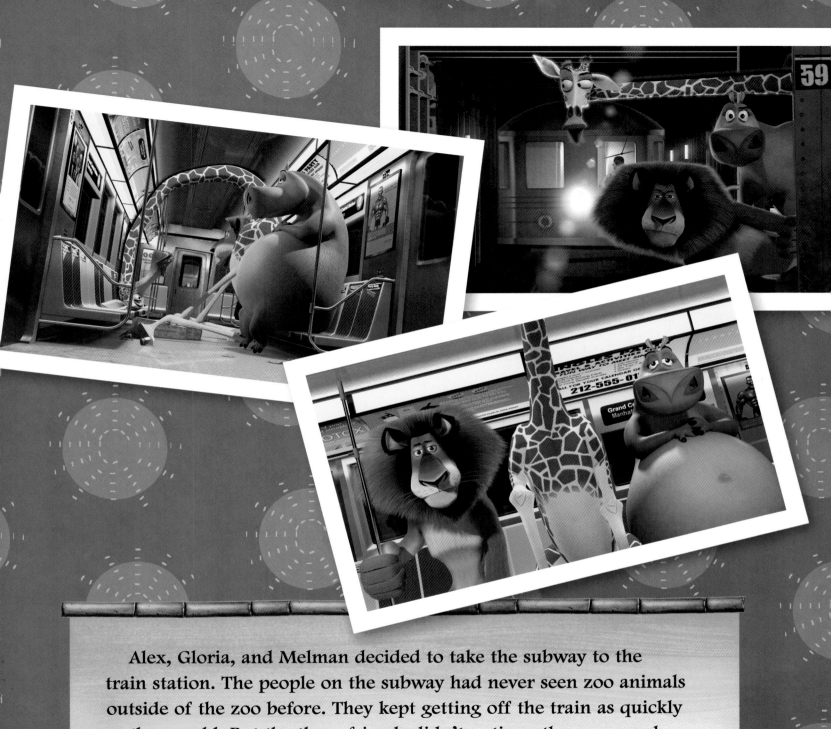

Alex, Gloria, and Melman decided to take the subway to the train station. The people on the subway had never seen zoo animals outside of the zoo before. They kept getting off the train as quickly as they could. But the three friends didn't notice—they were only thinking about finding Marty.

By the time Alex, Melman, and Gloria finally caught up with Marty at Grand Central Station, people were screaming and running everywhere. One brave old lady even attacked Alex as he ran toward Marty.

"Do you realize what you put us through?" asked Alex, shaking Marty. "Don't you ever, ever do this again!"

Suddenly there was a rumble.

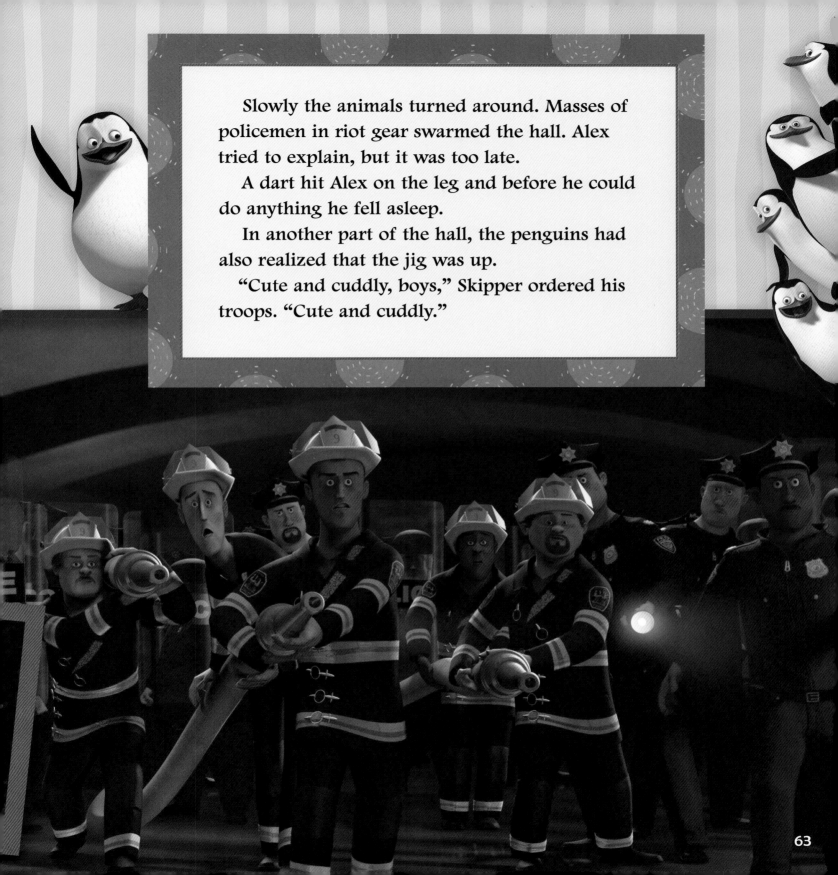

Slowly the animals turned around. Masses of policemen in riot gear swarmed the hall. Alex tried to explain, but it was too late.

A dart hit Alex on the leg and before he could do anything he fell asleep.

In another part of the hall, the penguins had also realized that the jig was up.

"Cute and cuddly, boys," Skipper ordered his troops. "Cute and cuddly."

The four friends woke up in wooden crates on a ship bound for Africa.

"It's a zoo transfer!" groaned Alex.

"Calm down," Marty cried. "Take it easy. We are going to be o-kizzay."

"No, Marty! We are not going to be o-kizzay. This is all your fault!" Alex shouted.

He and Marty began shoving at the walls of their crates, trying to push the other's over. All the crates began to rock back and forth.

Gloria asked, "Does anyone feel sick?"

"I feel sick," Melman moaned.

"Melman, you *always* feel sick," said Alex.

The penguins were also on the ship. Rico stuck his head out of an airhole and began to pick the lock on their crate. Soon the penguins were free.

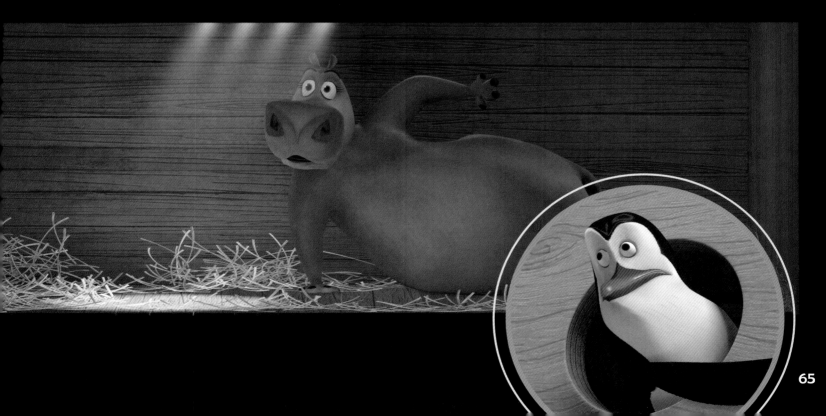

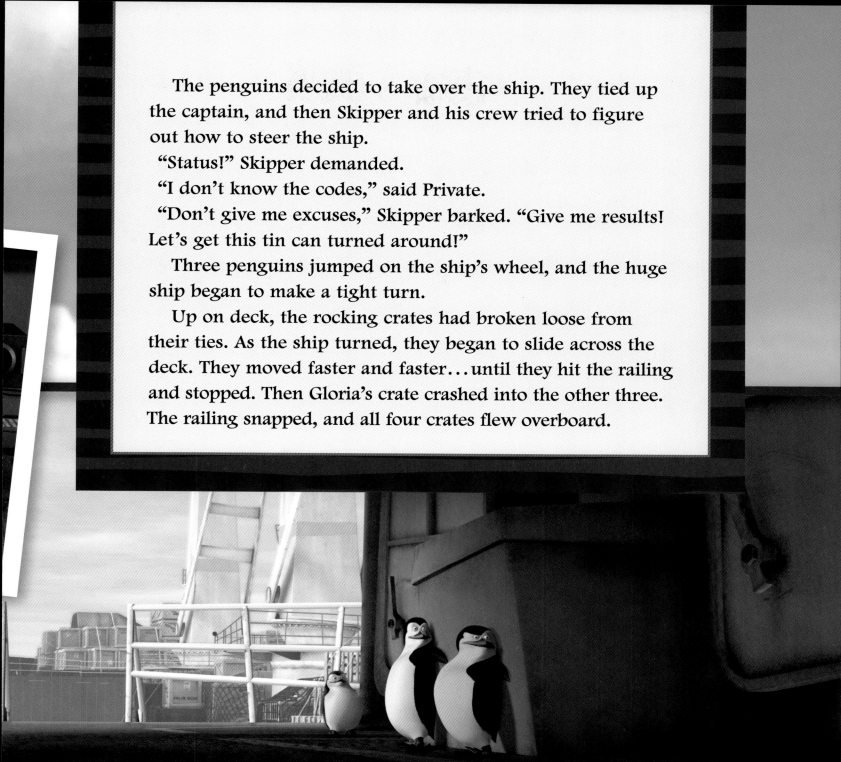

The penguins decided to take over the ship. They tied up the captain, and then Skipper and his crew tried to figure out how to steer the ship.

"Status!" Skipper demanded.

"I don't know the codes," said Private.

"Don't give me excuses," Skipper barked. "Give me results! Let's get this tin can turned around!"

Three penguins jumped on the ship's wheel, and the huge ship began to make a tight turn.

Up on deck, the rocking crates had broken loose from their ties. As the ship turned, they began to slide across the deck. They moved faster and faster...until they hit the railing and stopped. Then Gloria's crate crashed into the other three. The railing snapped, and all four crates flew overboard.

THE WILD

The crates floated and bobbed on the waves until they finally washed up on the shore. Alex, Gloria, Melman, and Marty were all back together. But where were they?

"San Diego," Melman announced. The others turned to stare at him. "White, sandy beaches, wide-open enclosures. This could be the San Diego Zoo."

"San Diego! What could be worse than San Diego?" Alex moaned.

But Marty liked what he saw. "This place is crack-a-lackin'!" he cried.

Gloria grabbed Alex before he could start chasing Marty and hung on tight. "We're just going to find the people," she said soothingly, "and get this mess straightened out!"

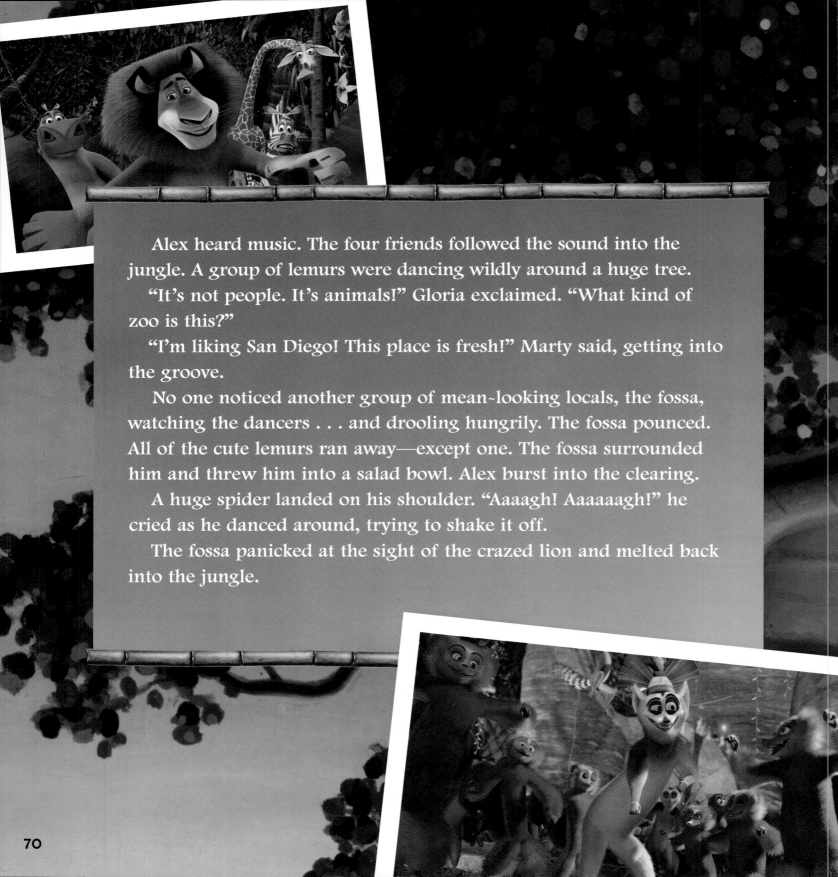

Alex heard music. The four friends followed the sound into the jungle. A group of lemurs were dancing wildly around a huge tree.

"It's not people. It's animals!" Gloria exclaimed. "What kind of zoo is this?"

"I'm liking San Diego! This place is fresh!" Marty said, getting into the groove.

No one noticed another group of mean-looking locals, the fossa, watching the dancers . . . and drooling hungrily. The fossa pounced. All of the cute lemurs ran away—except one. The fossa surrounded him and threw him into a salad bowl. Alex burst into the clearing.

A huge spider landed on his shoulder. "Aaaagh! Aaaaaagh!" he cried as he danced around, trying to shake it off.

The fossa panicked at the sight of the crazed lion and melted back into the jungle.

Gloria picked up Mort, the cute little lemur, and cuddled him. "Did the big, bad putty tat scare you?" she asked. Mort cooed at her.

Suddenly another lemur, Maurice, emerged from the jungle. He cleared his throat. "Presenting your Royal Highness, King Julien the thirteenth!"

Julien marched out of the bushes.

"He's got style," Marty whispered.

"What is he? A guinea pig?" Alex asked.

"Welcome," Julien said. "Welcome to the wild. We thank you with enormous gratitude for chasing away the fossa."

"The wild?" Alex shouted in disbelief.

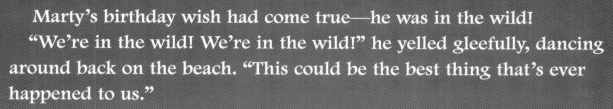

Marty's birthday wish had come true—he was in the wild!

"We're in the wild! We're in the wild!" he yelled gleefully, dancing around back on the beach. "This could be the best thing that's ever happened to us."

Alex didn't think so. In fact, he was sure that it was the worst thing that had ever, *ever* happened to him. All he could do was hope for a rescue boat.

Still on the ship, the penguins celebrated as they headed toward Antarctica. "Well, boys," Skipper exclaimed, "it's gonna be ice-cold sushi for breakfast!"

The penguins high-fived and settled down to some serious partying.

Alex had had it with Marty. Alex prowled down the beach and drew a line in the sand. "I've had enough of this! This is your side of the island and this is our side of the island, for those who love New York and care about going home."

"Fine," said Marty. "You all have your side, and I have mine. If you need me, I'll be over here, on the fun side of the island."

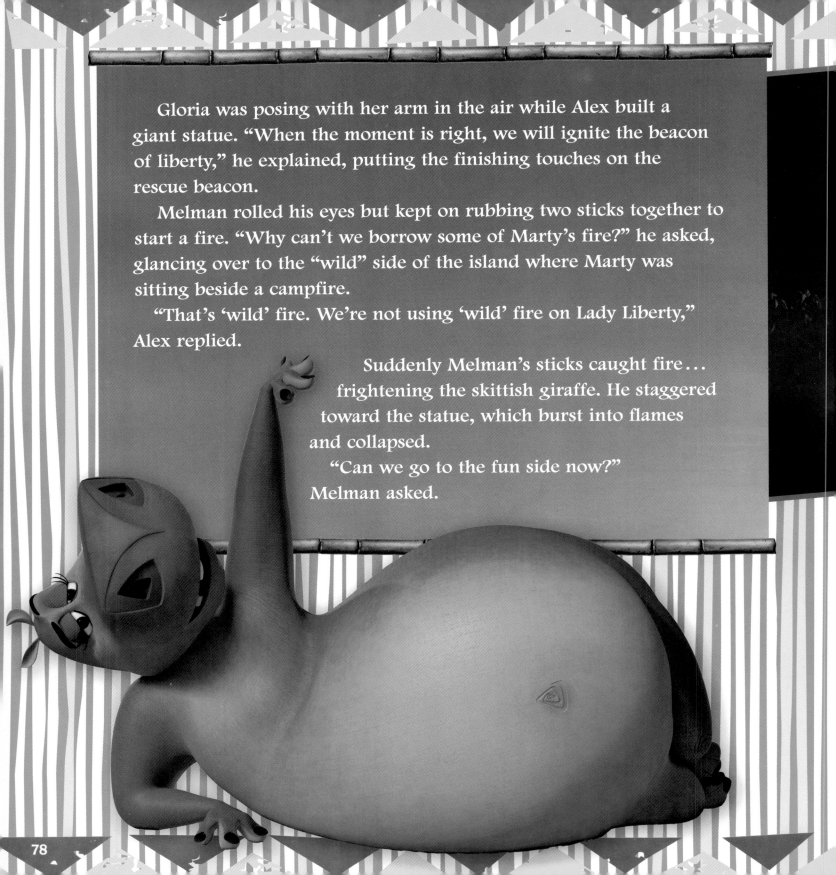

Gloria was posing with her arm in the air while Alex built a giant statue. "When the moment is right, we will ignite the beacon of liberty," he explained, putting the finishing touches on the rescue beacon.

Melman rolled his eyes but kept on rubbing two sticks together to start a fire. "Why can't we borrow some of Marty's fire?" he asked, glancing over to the "wild" side of the island where Marty was sitting beside a campfire.

"That's 'wild' fire. We're not using 'wild' fire on Lady Liberty," Alex replied.

Suddenly Melman's sticks caught fire... frightening the skittish giraffe. He staggered toward the statue, which burst into flames and collapsed.

"Can we go to the fun side now?" Melman asked.

Finally Alex gave in and went over to the fun side of the island. Gloria and Melman were already there, staying with Marty in his cozy hut.

"I've been kind of a jerk," Alex said to Marty. "If this is what you want, then I'll give it a shot."

"Welcome to *Casa del Wild*," smiled Marty.

Together again, the four friends spent the rest of the evening eating seaweed kabobs and stargazing.

The only thing that was missing was Alex's favorite food. Suddenly, he couldn't stop dreaming about steak. It was very strange.

The lemurs gathered to discuss the large animals who had arrived from New York.

"For as long as we can remember, we have been attacked and eaten," Julien said. "We will make the New York giants our friends. With Mr. Alex protecting us, we'll be safe and never have to worry about the dreaded fossa ever again!"

"Yay!" the lemurs shouted.

"I have a plan. The New York giants will wake up in paradise!" Julien yelled.

Meanwhile, the penguins had finally reached Antarctica—and they didn't like it. It was cold...very cold. So they headed back to the ship to look for someplace warm.

"Welcome to paradise!" Julien announced the next morning as the four friends gathered for a breakfast of fruits and vegetables—all supplied by the lemurs.

Alex, Marty, Gloria, and Melman looked around in amazement. They were standing in front of Marty's mural at the zoo...only this was real!

"How about once around the park?" Marty asked. "Who's with me?"

Alex suddenly took off running, with Marty in hot pursuit. The pair ran through the wild, tackling each other and having fun. But something strange was happening to Alex. By the time they returned to the waterhole, Alex was feeling better—and wilder—than he'd ever felt before.

After breakfast, Marty introduced Alex for a show unlike any he had ever performed in the New York zoo. "Ladies and gentlemen. Primates of all ages. The wild proudly presents the king...Alex the lion!"

Alex leaped up onto a rock and, for the first time in his life, really ROARED!

"Whoa," said Gloria. "I never heard that before."

The locals began cheering and doing the wave. Alex threw his arms in the air...*Shing!*...Claws popped out of his paws.

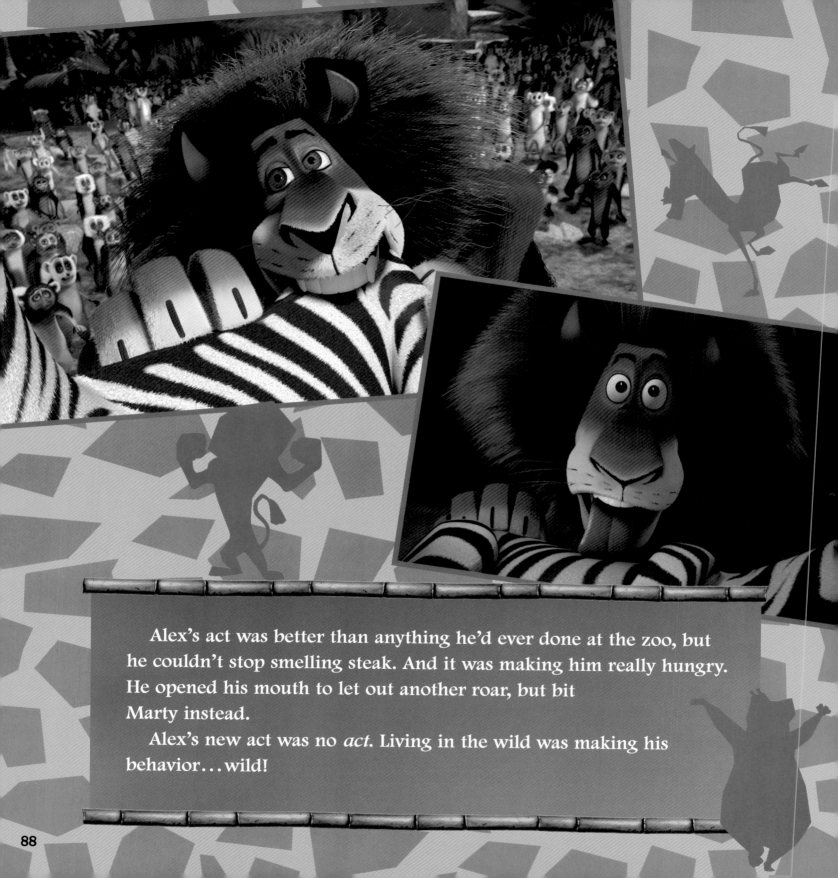

Alex's act was better than anything he'd ever done at the zoo, but he couldn't stop smelling steak. And it was making him really hungry. He opened his mouth to let out another roar, but bit Marty instead.

Alex's new act was no *act*. Living in the wild was making his behavior...wild!

There was only one thing to do.

"Your friend is what you'd call a deluxe model hunting-and-eating machine," Julien explained. "Mr. Alex belongs with his own kind, on the fossa side of the island."

Everyone stared at Alex, who began to back away into the jungle until he disappeared.

Marty was confused. "This isn't how the wild is supposed to be," he said as he stared after his friend.

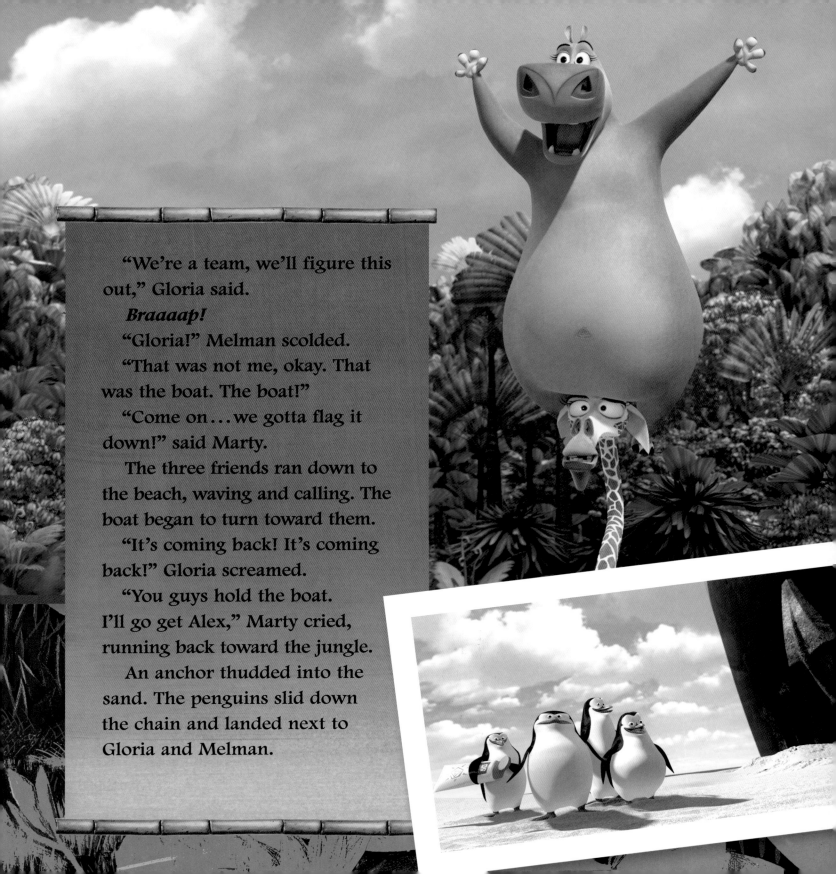

"We're a team, we'll figure this out," Gloria said.

Braaaap!

"Gloria!" Melman scolded.

"That was not me, okay. That was the boat. The boat!"

"Come on...we gotta flag it down!" said Marty.

The three friends ran down to the beach, waving and calling. The boat began to turn toward them.

"It's coming back! It's coming back!" Gloria screamed.

"You guys hold the boat. I'll go get Alex," Marty cried, running back toward the jungle.

An anchor thudded into the sand. The penguins slid down the chain and landed next to Gloria and Melman.

Marty finally found Alex, sleeping in a homemade lion hut.

"Alex! The boat is here! We can go home!"

"Stay away!" Alex said. "I'm a monster."

"No you're not," replied Marty. "You're the best friend a guy could have, and I'm not leaving without you."

But Alex just went back into his hut.

While Marty and Alex had been talking, the fossa had been gathering. When Alex went back inside, they began to pour down from the rocks to surround the zebra.

Marty took one look at the hungry fossa and began running, and calling for Alex. But there were too many fossa. He was trapped.

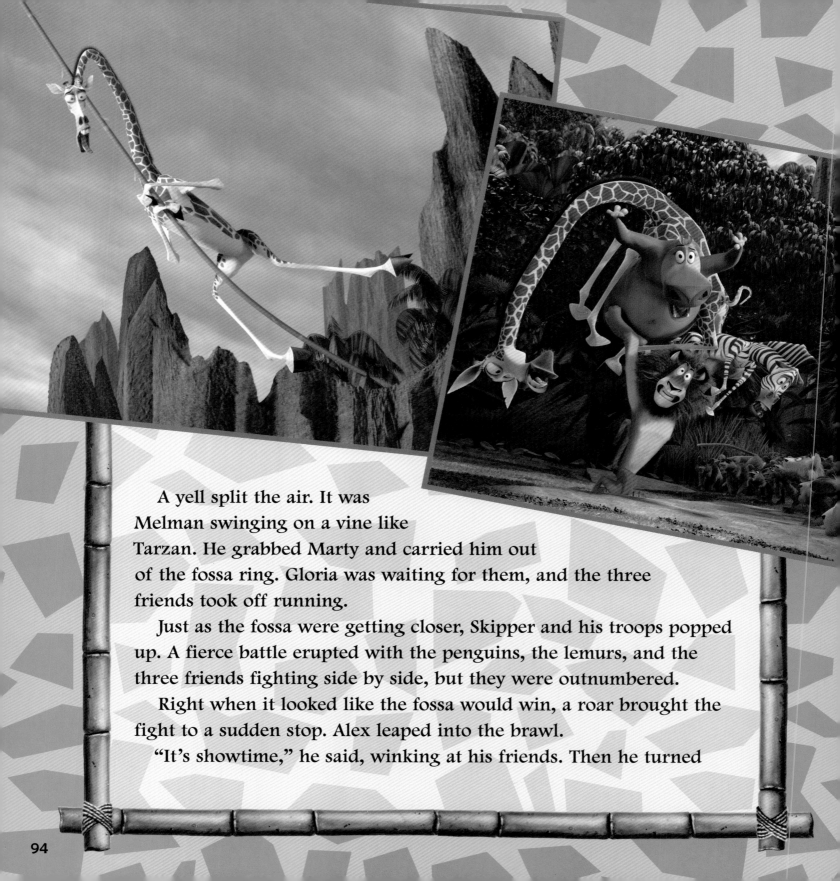

A yell split the air. It was
Melman swinging on a vine like
Tarzan. He grabbed Marty and carried him out
of the fossa ring. Gloria was waiting for them, and the three
friends took off running.

Just as the fossa were getting closer, Skipper and his troops popped
up. A fierce battle erupted with the penguins, the lemurs, and the
three friends fighting side by side, but they were outnumbered.

Right when it looked like the fossa would win, a roar brought the
fight to a sudden stop. Alex leaped into the brawl.

"It's showtime," he said, winking at his friends. Then he turned to face the fossa. "I never, ever want to see you on my turf again!" He roared at the terrified fossa, who didn't wait any longer. They turned and *ran* to the other side of the island.

That night, there was a huge party to celebrate. Music played, and the penguins made sushi. Alex ate some. It wasn't steak, but he liked it a lot.

As the four friends looked around at the locals and the penguins, they realized that it didn't matter where they were as long as they were together. Marty's dream of living in the wild had come true. And he and Alex were friends again. Things couldn't get any better. With that they all raised their coconut cups in a toast.

he Vikings of Berk Island were used to nightly attacks of flaming fireballs. After all, they had been fighting dragons for seven generations.

One teenager, Hiccup, wasn't a typical Viking. Where most were brawny, Hiccup was brainy. But that didn't stop him longing to be like the others.

When he wasn't helping Gobber in the blacksmith's workshop, Hiccup was busy inventing weapons to bring down the dragons that attacked nightly.

"Man the fort, they need me out there!" Gobber ordered Hiccup one night, as he prepared to join the battle.

Hiccup realized that this was the perfect opportunity to try out his latest invention—the Mangler. If he could bring down a dragon, he was sure his father, Stoick the Vast, would finally let him join the other teenagers in dragon training.

As the dragons rampaged through the village, Hiccup carefully took aim...and fired. The Mangler's bola whizzed through the air toward a deadly Night Fury. To Hiccup's amazement, it hit the giant beast and brought it down.

Before Hiccup had the chance to celebrate, a Monstrous Nightmare chased him through the village.

Luckily Stoick was there to rescue his son.

The next day, Hiccup set off in search of the Night Fury that he had brought down. He found the injured dragon lying in the woods, but Hiccup couldn't bring himself to kill it. "Who am I kidding?" he asked, as he untied the bola from the creature's damaged tail.

Suddenly, the mighty beast jumped on Hiccup's chest and let out a huge roar. It could have killed him there and then, but instead the Night Fury flew off, clumsily.

Later, Hiccup came across the dragon in a small cove. He realized he wasn't able to fly properly because of his damaged tail, so Hiccup started sketching ideas for a new invention.

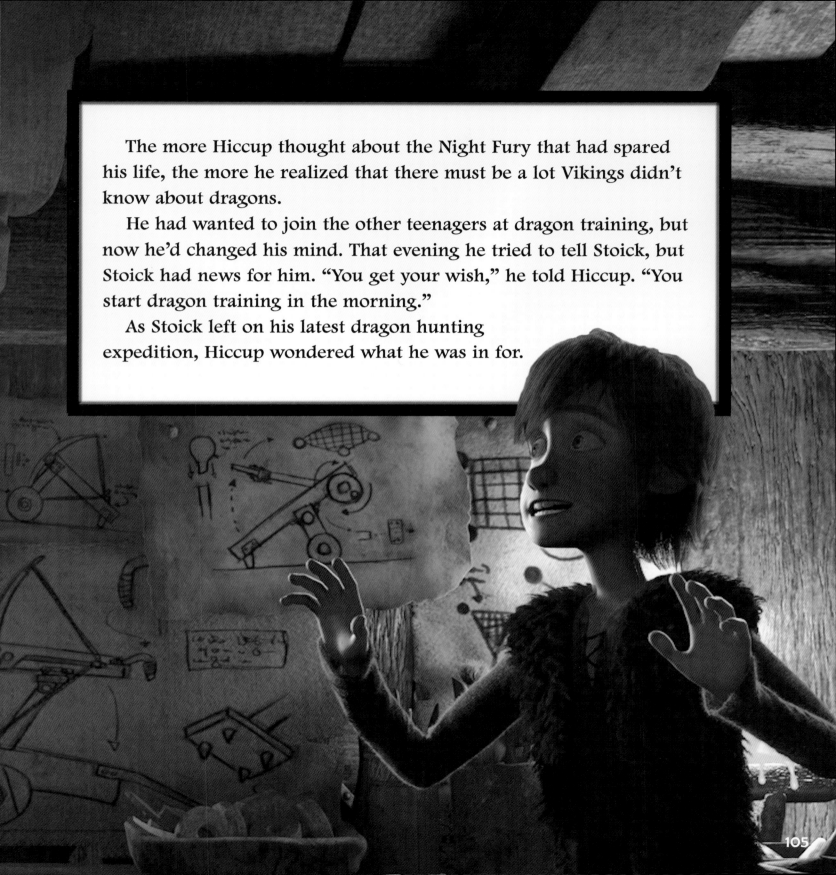

The more Hiccup thought about the Night Fury that had spared his life, the more he realized that there must be a lot Vikings didn't know about dragons.

He had wanted to join the other teenagers at dragon training, but now he'd changed his mind. That evening he tried to tell Stoick, but Stoick had news for him. "You get your wish," he told Hiccup. "You start dragon training in the morning."

As Stoick left on his latest dragon hunting expedition, Hiccup wondered what he was in for.

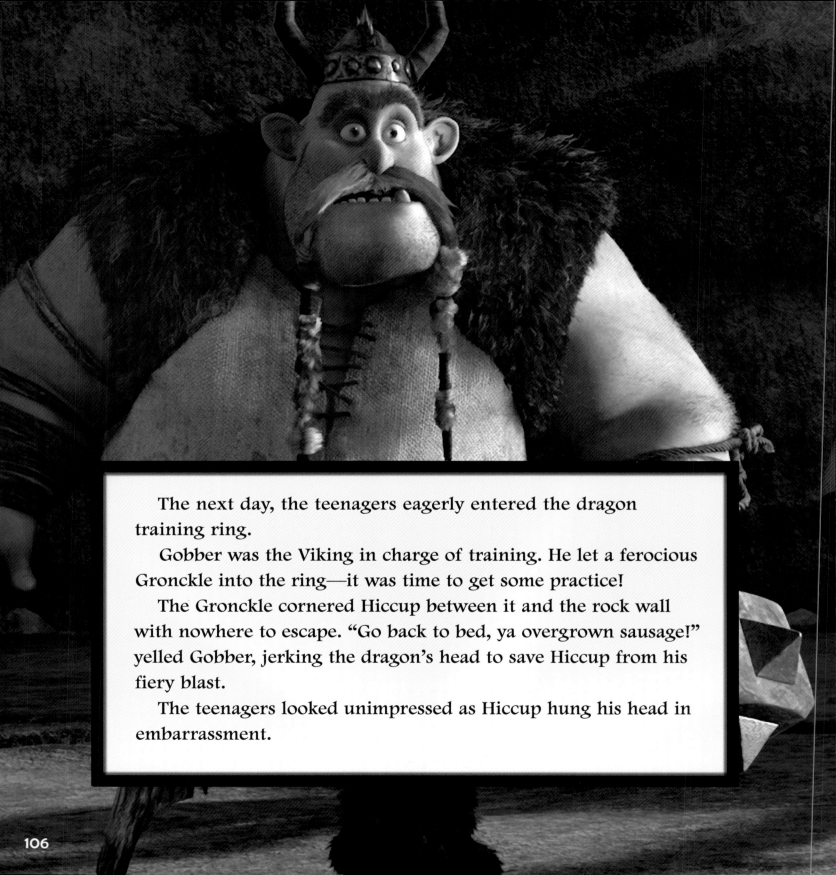

The next day, the teenagers eagerly entered the dragon training ring.

Gobber was the Viking in charge of training. He let a ferocious Gronckle into the ring—it was time to get some practice!

The Gronckle cornered Hiccup between it and the rock wall with nowhere to escape. "Go back to bed, ya overgrown sausage!" yelled Gobber, jerking the dragon's head to save Hiccup from his fiery blast.

The teenagers looked unimpressed as Hiccup hung his head in embarrassment.

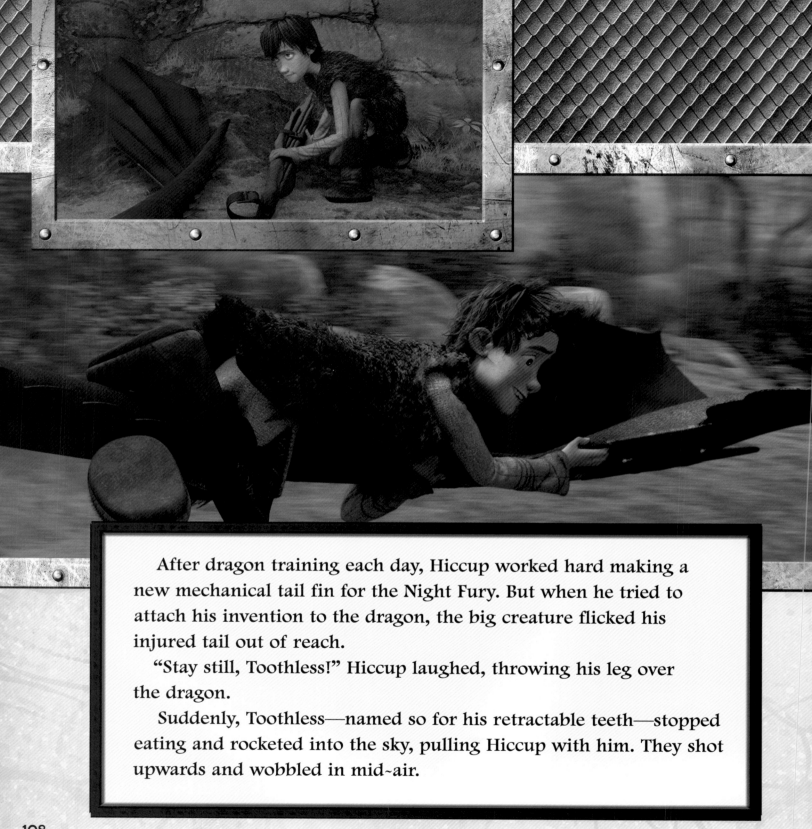

After dragon training each day, Hiccup worked hard making a new mechanical tail fin for the Night Fury. But when he tried to attach his invention to the dragon, the big creature flicked his injured tail out of reach.

"Stay still, Toothless!" Hiccup laughed, throwing his leg over the dragon.

Suddenly, Toothless—named so for his retractable teeth—stopped eating and rocketed into the sky, pulling Hiccup with him. They shot upwards and wobbled in mid-air.

"AAAAGGGHHHH!" yelled poor Hiccup, as they hurtled over the water, landing in the waves with a massive splash.

Hiccup changed his design and the next time he strapped on the tail fin it worked perfectly.

"We're flying!" cheered Hiccup as they soared through the sky.

Every day, training grew harder and harder for the young Vikings. They fought Gronckles and Deadly Nadders. They tried to outwit Zipplebacks and Terrible Terrors. They battled with axes, swords and shields. They learned how many shots of fire each dragon had, where to stand, and how to attack!

When training was over, Hiccup made sure nobody saw him as he crept down to the cove to see Toothless. His new friend taught him some dragon facts of his own such as where dragons enjoy being tickled and which fish they don't like to eat, especially eels.

It was much more fun than fighting.

Hiccup used his new-found dragon knowledge to his advantage in the ring. During the next training session, Gobber released a Zippleback. It charged towards the teenagers creating huge fiery explosions. Hiccup ran towards the dragon and secretly showed him a smelly eel! The Zippleback backed away with a horrified snort while Hiccup grinned.

Gobber and the teenagers thought Hiccup had power over the dragons! Suddenly, everyone started looking at Hiccup differently. None of them guessed what had really happened!

When Stoick returned from his expedition, he heard all about Hiccup's success in the ring. "You really had me going there," he told Hiccup. "Fifteen years of the worst Viking Berk has ever seen! It was rough. I almost gave up on you!"

Hiccup smiled awkwardly as Stoick handed his son a huge Viking helmet.

"I, um…brought you something," Stoick said gruffly. "It will keep you safe in the ring."

"Wow. Thanks," replied Hiccup holding the heavy helmet.

Stoick tapped his own helmet and smiled. "Matching set," he said proudly.

Astrid, one of the other teenagers at dragon training, began to notice that Hiccup spent a lot of time on his own. One day, she followed him to the cove and discovered him with the Night Fury!

Hiccup convinced Astrid to go for a ride on Toothless and they flew toward a distant island surrounded by fog. Dozens of dragons were flying toward the island, carrying food they'd stolen from Berk.

Suddenly, Hiccup and Astrid saw a monstrous, six-eyed beast! It was the Red Death! The teenagers realized that the dragons were feeding the Red Death so he didn't eat *them*.

Finally, they discovered why the dragons attacked their village!

On the day of Hiccup's final dragon training test, his secret friendship with Toothless was revealed. Hiccup watched helplessly as Stoick captured the Night Fury and dragged him away.

Hiccup tried to explain about the Red Death.

"The dragons raid us because they have to!" he cried. But Stoick wouldn't listen. Now that he knew about Dragon Island, he was determined to kill every last dragon. Stoick rounded up the adults and set sail, forcing Toothless to be his guide.

Hiccup quickly gathered the teenagers. "I need your help!" he cried.

If only Stoick had listened to Hiccup before he set sail. The Red Death was like no dragon the adults had ever seen. He crushed their weapons like egg shells and blasted holes in their ships. The Vikings were losing the battle!

Suddenly, the teenagers swooped to the rescue, riding the dragons they'd been taught to fight!

Hiccup saved Toothless from Stoick's sinking ship and the pair bravely joined the battle, fighting to defend the adults. Stoick saw that Hiccup had been right all along. The dragons weren't the problem—it was the Red Death who was their real enemy!

An angry shot of fire burst out of the Red Death's mouth, demolishing another ship.

"It's unstoppable!" Gobber cried.

Gobber's words gave Hiccup an idea. "What do you say we do things our way?" he whispered to Toothless.

After blasting the giant beast's wings full of holes, Toothless and Hiccup flew in front of the dragon so he would chase them, then they dropped into a nose dive towards the ground. The Red Death followed, fiery gas hissing from his mouth. Toothless let out a sonic blast. The Red Death couldn't stop. He swallowed the flames and exploded as he crashed helplessly to the ground!

Hiccup's idea worked. They had destroyed the Red Death! But Hiccup's glory came at a price—he was injured in the fight.

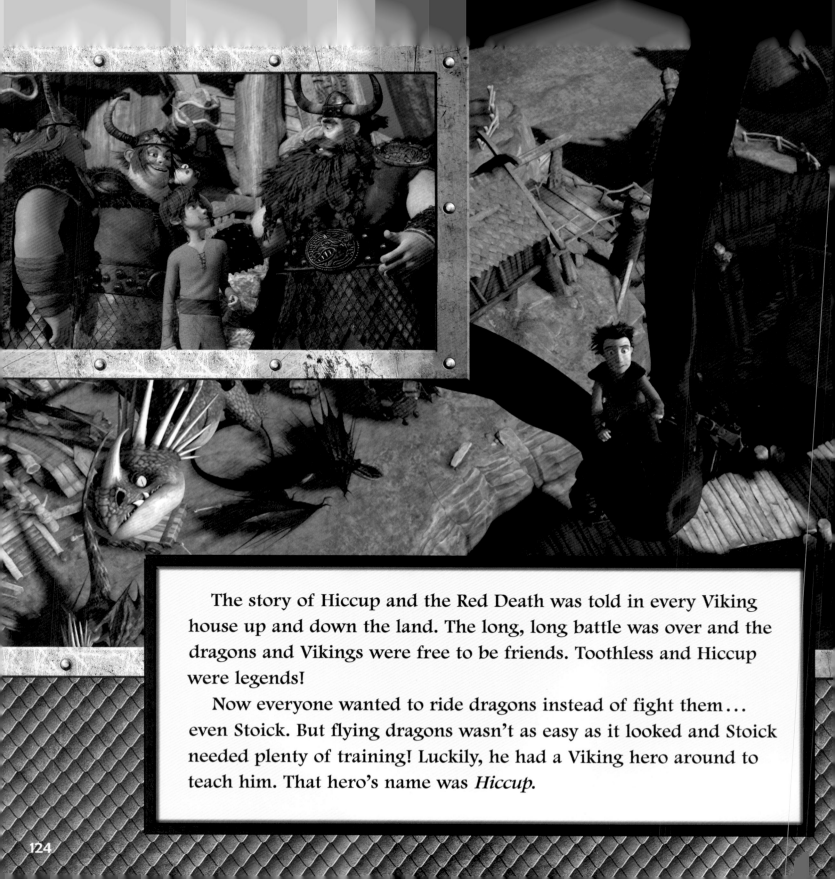

The story of Hiccup and the Red Death was told in every Viking house up and down the land. The long, long battle was over and the dragons and Vikings were free to be friends. Toothless and Hiccup were legends!

Now everyone wanted to ride dragons instead of fight them... even Stoick. But flying dragons wasn't as easy as it looked and Stoick needed plenty of training! Luckily, he had a Viking hero around to teach him. That hero's name was *Hiccup*.

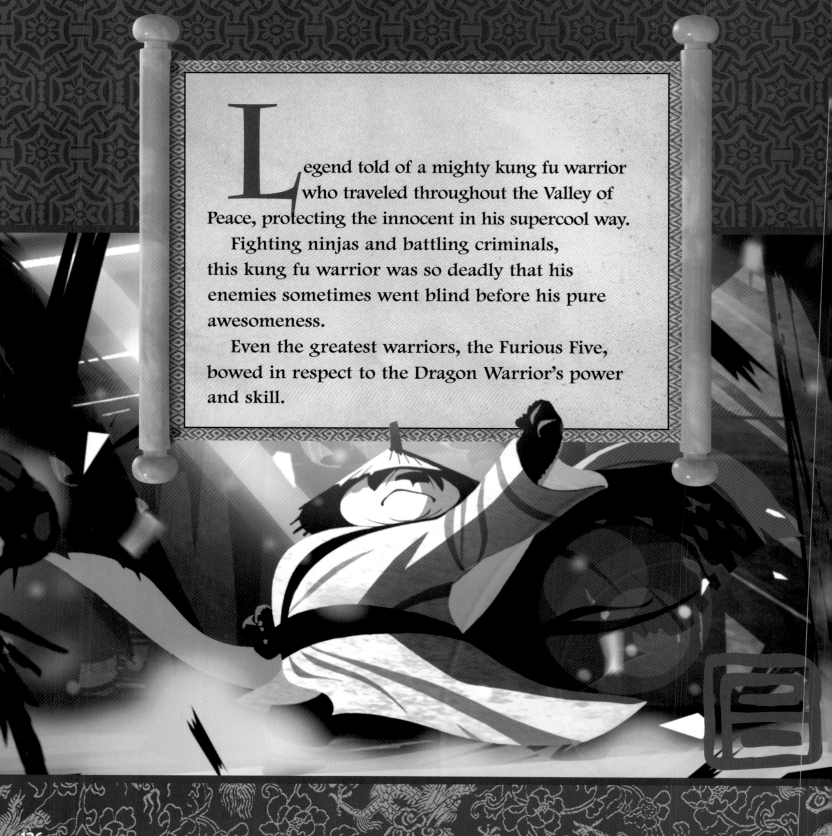

Legend told of a mighty kung fu warrior who traveled throughout the Valley of Peace, protecting the innocent in his supercool way.

Fighting ninjas and battling criminals, this kung fu warrior was so deadly that his enemies sometimes went blind before his pure awesomeness.

Even the greatest warriors, the Furious Five, bowed in respect to the Dragon Warrior's power and skill.

127

"Po! Get up! You'll be late for work!" Po's father yelled up the stairs.

Po sat up in bed. He had been dreaming! He wasn't the Dragon Warrior after all. He was just a large, sleepy panda.

He rushed downstairs to his father's noodle shop. The shop was crowded with customers who loved his father's secret-ingredient noodle soup. As Po struggled to squeeze and fit between the tables, he was still thinking about his dream. It would be so great to be a real kung fu warrior who sent his enemies flying.

Oops! Po's belly sent the tables in the noodle shop flying instead.

Meanwhile, at the Jade Palace, Shifu was training the Furious Five when Master Oogway summoned him.

"I have had a vision," Oogway said. "Tai Lung will return."

Tai Lung had once been Shifu's star pupil but he had grown overly ambitious. When he tried to steal the Dragon Scroll and its secret to unlimited power, Oogway and Shifu had stopped him. Now, Tai Lung had been locked away in prison for years.

Shifu was concerned—he knew that Oogway's visions were never wrong. It was time to plan for Tai Lung's return.

Word of the plan spread quickly. That very day, Oogway would choose the Dragon Warrior—the mighty kung fu master destined to save the Valley from Tai Lung.

"This is the greatest day in kung fu history!" Po cried when he heard the news. He had to be there to see which of the Furious Five would be chosen.

He ran up the arena stairs with all his might, panting and sweating. He finally reached the top, just to see the doors slam in his face—*whoosh!* He tried to pole-vault over the wall. Then he tried to climb. But *nothing* worked ...until he shot himself into the air with some fireworks.

SPLAT!

Po landed inside the arena. When he looked up, he saw that Master Oogway was pointing at him. Master Shifu and the Furious Five were staring down at him.

"The universe has brought us the Dragon Warrior," Oogway declared.

The crowd cheered in celebration of the news.

"What?" Po said in surprise.

"What?" exclaimed Shifu and the Five in disbelief.

Soon, Po found himself in the Sacred Hall of Heroes. It was the coolest place he'd ever seen. Ancient kung fu artifacts were displayed throughout the room. Po ran around checking out all of them.

"Hel~loooo!" he called into the Urn of Whispering Warriors.

"Have you finished sightseeing?" a voice asked.

Po gasped. The urn was talking to him!

"Would you turn around?" the voice said.

Po turned around. "Master Shifu!" he cried when he saw the kung fu master. So *that* was who was talking to him! Po was so surprised that he bumped into the urn. It shattered into dozens of tiny pieces. "Um, do you have some glue?" he asked sheepishly.

Shifu wasn't at all impressed with this new so-called Dragon Warrior. He tested Po by putting him into the Wuxi Finger Hold.

It really, really hurt. But Po still thought it was pretty cool.

Shifu took Po to the training hall where the Five were practicing. Masters Tigress, Monkey, Crane, Viper, and Mantis performed death-defying kung fu stunts. Po was thrilled to see his heroes in action.

Po was less thrilled when he realized *he* was supposed to join in.

"Go ahead, panda," Shifu said. "Show us what you can do."

Po was flung into the gauntlet as, *OUCH!* a spiky tethered ball sent him flying into the jade exercise, which *OOF!* spilled him into the army of wooden dummies, when *UGH!* he got whacked for a final time, landing beaten-up in front of the disapproving Five.

Po didn't fit in at the training hall, and he didn't fit in at the Furious Five's bunkhouse. None of the Five wanted him around. They didn't think he was worthy of being the Dragon Warrior.

Feeling dejected, Po wandered outside to a peach tree. How could Shifu ever turn someone like *him* into a kung fu hero?

"Maybe I should just quit and go back to making noodles," he mumbled sadly.

Master Oogway overheard the panda's sad words and gave him some advice. "Yesterday is history, tomorrow is a mystery, but today is a gift. That is why it is the present," said Oogway.

Po smiled. He was willing to try again.

Meanwhile, an impenetrable prison stood far away from the Jade Palace. It had a thousand guards and only one prisoner—the dangerous snow leopard Tai Lung.

Tai Lung had waited years for his chance to escape. The time was now—and he was ready. He used a stray feather to pick the lock on his armor.

The guards didn't stand a chance against his powerful kung fu leaps and kicks. Tai Lung dodged spears and clawed up the rocky walls to burst out of the prison.

At last, he was free! Now he could return to the palace and claim his rightful title of Dragon Warrior!

Back at the palace, Po was training hard with the Five. First Viper flipped him ears over heels and sent him crashing down on his head.

"That was awesome!" Po cried. "Let's go again!"

Next it was Monkey's turn. He whacked Po all over his chubby body with a bamboo cane. Then Crane sent Po falling flat on his face.

Shifu was fed up. "I've been taking it easy on you, panda," he said. "Your next opponent will be...me!"

He grabbed Po in a kung fu hold. "The path to victory is to use your opponent's strength against him until he fails or quits," he said.

Po was inspired. "Don't worry, Master. I will never quit!"

But time was running out for Po to master kung fu. The bad news about Tai Lung's escape reached the palace. Shifu rushed to tell Oogway.

"That *is* bad news," Oogway said. *"If* you do not believe that the Dragon Warrior can stop him."

"Master, that panda is not the Dragon Warrior!" Shifu cried.

"You just need to believe, Shifu," Oogway told him. "Now you must continue your journey without me."

He handed his staff to Shifu. Then he backed away and disappeared forever in a swirl of petals.

Back at the bunkhouse, Po was making the Furious Five laugh by imitating Shifu when Shifu himself suddenly walked in.

"Tai Lung is coming," he told Po sternly. "You are the only one who can stop him."

"What?" Po cried. He laughed nervously. "And here I thought you had no sense of humor. *I'm* going to stop Tai Lung?"

But he realized Shifu was serious. As soon as the master turned to speak to the Five, Po spun on his heel and ran away as fast as he could. Shifu soon caught up with Po. His message was clear.

"I can train you," Shifu said. "I will turn you into the Dragon Warrior."

Tigress was sure Po could never defeat Tai Lung. She sneaked out of the bunkhouse that night to do the job herself. The others chased after her.

"Don't try to stop me," she warned them.

"We're not trying to stop you," Viper said. "We're coming with you!"

The Furious Five found Tai Lung on a rope bridge spanning a vast gorge.
The Five began their attack. They fought bravely, just as Shifu had taught them.

But the snow leopard's strong muscles backed up his kung fu kicks as he overpowered the group, finally using a special kung fu nerve attack that froze them in place. Tai Lung snarled as he bounded away to the Valley.

Back at the palace, Shifu found Po eating everything he could get his paws on. Finally Shifu understood. *This* was the key to the panda's greatness!

Shifu changed his training plans. He would use food not to motivate Po—but to activate him! Instead of the usual kung fu methods, he used stir-fry and dumplings to build and refine Po's skills.

It worked! Po got better and better.

Po was excited. His kung fu dreams were coming true at last. Maybe he *was* worthy of being the Dragon Warrior after all!

The Five returned, dejected, and told Shifu of their defeat to Tai Lung. Shifu decided that Po needed to meet his destiny head-on—he needed the Dragon Scroll.

"Read it, Po, and fulfill your destiny," he said. "Read it and become the Dragon Warrior!"

Po unrolled the scroll and gasped. "It's blank!"

All his new confidence seeped away. Tai Lung had already defeated the Five. How was a chubby, noodle-slurping panda ever supposed to beat him? Even Shifu didn't understand.

When Shifu ordered an evacuation of the Valley, Po went straight to his father's noodle shop. His father quickly realized that Po needed some encouragement. And so he finally revealed the secret ingredient in his special noodle soup.

"There *is* no secret ingredient," he told Po. "To make something special, you just have to *believe* it's special."

Po was shocked. "There is no secret ingredient," he said to himself.

He unrolled the blank scroll again and saw his own reflection in the shiny surface. It all made sense—there *was* no secret of the scroll. Now Po understood what he had to do!

When Tai Lung arrived at the palace, Shifu was waiting for him.
"I have come home, Master," Tai Lung said.
"This is no longer your home," Shifu replied. "And I am no longer your master."

They began a fierce fight. Shifu was a great kung fu master, but Tai Lung was now too strong for him.

Po burst into the palace just as Tai Lung was about to make a final, deadly move on Shifu. At first Tai Lung couldn't believe it: *This* chubby panda was the Dragon Warrior?

"What are you going to do, big guy?" he taunted. "Sit on me?"

But Po didn't use the same kung fu moves as other warriors...he had his own panda style. The battle raged down the palace steps and through the village. The panda bounced the bad guy off his big belly.

When the dust settled, Po jumped up and snatched Tai Lung's finger.

"Not the Wuxi Finger Hold!" yelled Tai Lung. The panda flexed his pinky and it was all over. The Dragon Warrior had won.

Cheers rang out from every direction as Po marched victoriously through the Valley.

Shifu could hardly believe it. "It is as Oogway foretold," he said. "You are the Dragon Warrior. Thank you, Po!" The Five bowed with respect.

Po couldn't stop smiling. It was great that everyone finally believed he was truly the Dragon Warrior. But it was even better believing in himself!

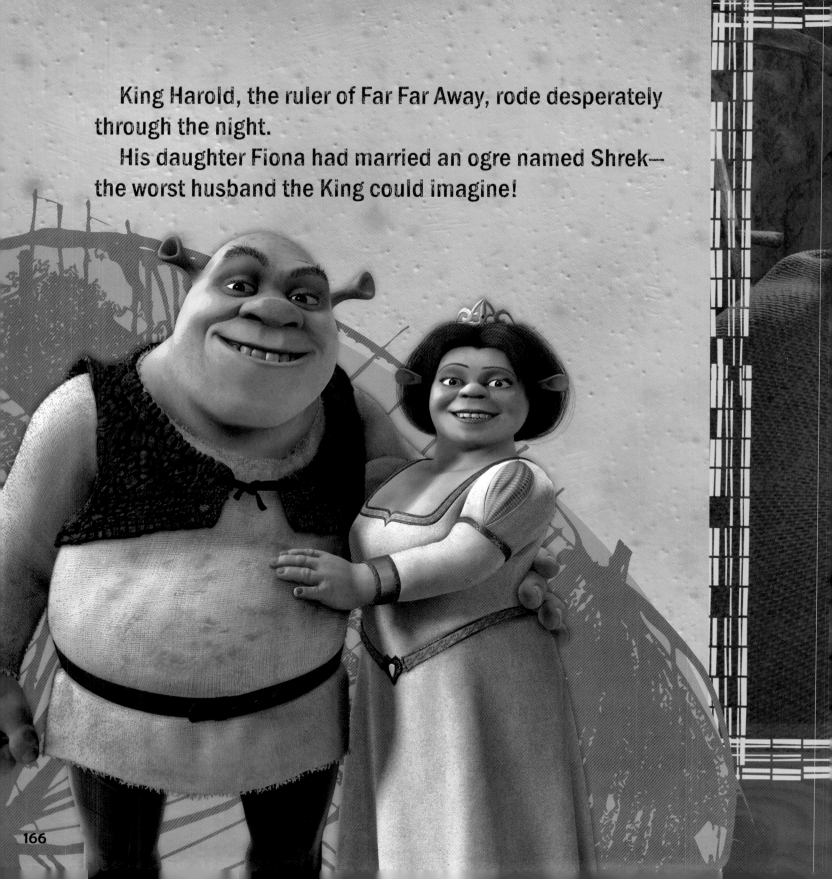

King Harold, the ruler of Far Far Away, rode desperately through the night.

His daughter Fiona had married an ogre named Shrek— the worst husband the King could imagine!

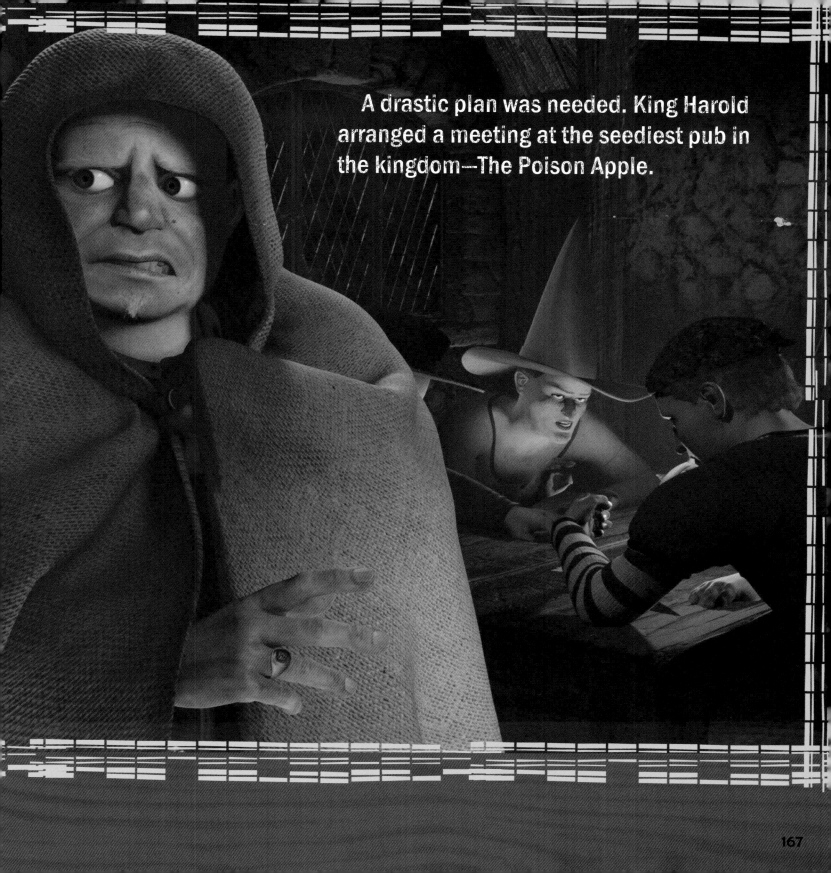

A drastic plan was needed. King Harold arranged a meeting at the seediest pub in the kingdom---The Poison Apple.

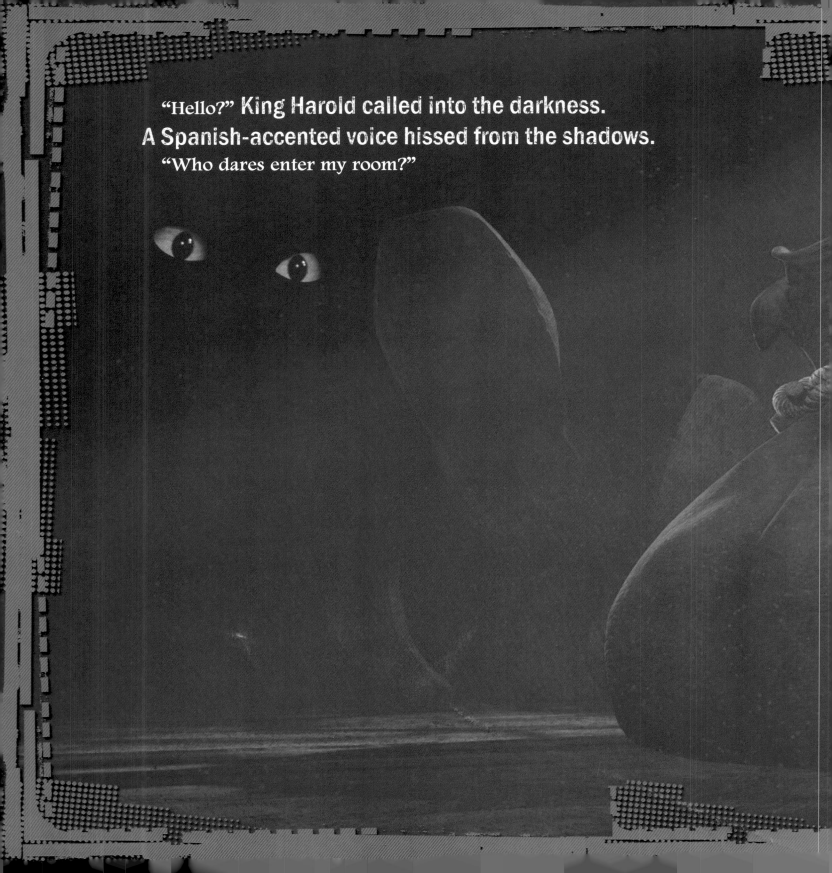

"Hello?" King Harold called into the darkness.
A Spanish-accented voice hissed from the shadows.
"Who dares enter my room?"

"I hope I'm not interrupting," said the King, staring into a pair of bright green eyes, "but I'm told you're the one to talk to about an *ogre problem.*"

The eyes narrowed.

"You are correct. But for this I charge a great deal of money."

"Would this be enough?" King Harold dropped a bulging bag of gold onto the table.

The stranger's hiss turned into a purr. "Tell me where I can find this ogre."

At dawn the next morning, Shrek and Donkey found themselves wandering in circles through the forest.

"Face it, Donkey," said Shrek. "We're lost."

"We can't be lost," insisted Donkey. "The King told us to meet him for a hunt right here—"

"—in the deepest, darkest part of the woods!" Donkey paused to shiver. "Yeah, right by those sinister trees with those scary-looking branches."

"Great," complained Shrek. "My one chance to fix things with Fiona's dad, and I end up lost in the woods with *you*."

"Don't get all huffy with me!" said Donkey. "You were the one who didn't want to stop and get directions! I'm only trying to help."

Shrek sighed. "I know. I'm sorry, all right?"

Then Shrek heard a strange sound. He glanced down at Donkey, who smiled up at him. "Donkey, I know we just shared a tender moment, but what's up with the purring?"

"Man, what are you talking about?" demanded Donkey. "I ain't purring. Donkeys don't purr."

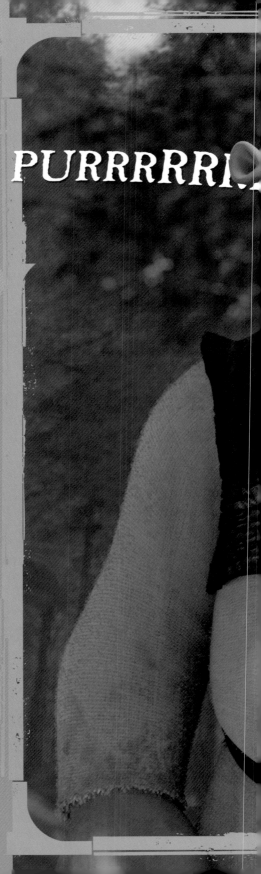

PURRRRRI

A dashing figure leaped out from behind a tree. "Ha ha!" cried the stranger. "Fear me...if you dare!" He let out a horrible hiss that made Donkey's fur stand on end.

"Look out!" Donkey shouted as he saw the stranger's sword. "He's got a piece!"

But Shrek only grinned. "It's a cat, Donkey," he said.

"C'mere, little kitty, kitty, kitty…"

With a vicious snarl, the cat attacked! But he
didn't use his sword. He pounced out of his big
boots, scratching Shrek with his razor-sharp claws.

Shrek howled in pain. "Ow! Ow! Get it off!" He
jumped around in a frenzy, trying to grab the hissing,
clawing ball of fur.

Donkey crouched, ready to kick. "Hold still!" he
told Shrek.

BOOF!

Donkey kicked with all his might! He missed the cat. But he nailed Shrek. The cat sprang loose.

Shrek doubled over in pain.

"Donnnn…keeeey…" he groaned.

With Shrek down, the dashing feline jumped back into his big boots and drew his sword with a flourish. "Now, ye ogre, pray for mercy from…

PUSS IN BOOTS!"

Before he could continue his attack, Puss In Boots began to gag.

He gasped and spit. "Heh heh. Hairball," he said sheepishly.

Donkey glanced down at the mess on the ground. "Oh, that is *nasty*!"

Shrek grabbed Puss In Boots by the scruff of the neck.

"Oh, *madre*!" Puss cried, terrified. "Please! I implore you! It was nothing personal, *señor*! The King paid me much gold to hunt you down and—"

"Whoa!" interrupted Shrek. "*Fiona's father* paid you to kill me?"

"The rich King?" asked Puss In Boots. "*Sí.*"

Shrek dropped the cat on his tail. "So much for one big happy family."

Donkey could see how much this news hurt his friend. "Aw, c'mon, Shrek, don't feel bad. Almost everybody who meets you wants to kill you."

"Just because I'm not Prince Charming?" asked Shrek sadly.

"*Si,* that is exactly what the King said," confirmed Puss In Boots.

"It's not like I wouldn't change if I could," sighed Shrek.

"Into a prince?" hooted Donkey. "That would take a miracle!"

Shrek's eyes lit up. "We could go visit Fairy Godmother—maybe *she* can help me find my Happily Ever After. Are you up for a little quest, Donkey?"

Donkey grinned. "All *right!* Shrek and Donkey on another whirlwind adventure!"

Puss In Boots jumped to his feet. "Stop!" he said. "Ogre, I have misjudged you. On my honor, I will stay with you until I have saved your life as you have spared mine!"

Donkey wasn't impressed. "I'm sorry, the position of annoying talking animal has already been taken," he said. "Let's go, Shrek."

But Shrek smiled at the cat, who was looking up at him with wide, adorable eyes. "Aw, c'mon, Donkey. Look at him in his wee little boots. How many cats can wear boots? Let's keep him."

Donkey was stunned. "Say what?" Shaking his head in disbelief, Donkey marched away.

"Oh…listen," said Shrek. "He's purring!"

"Oh, so now it's cute?" grumbled Donkey.

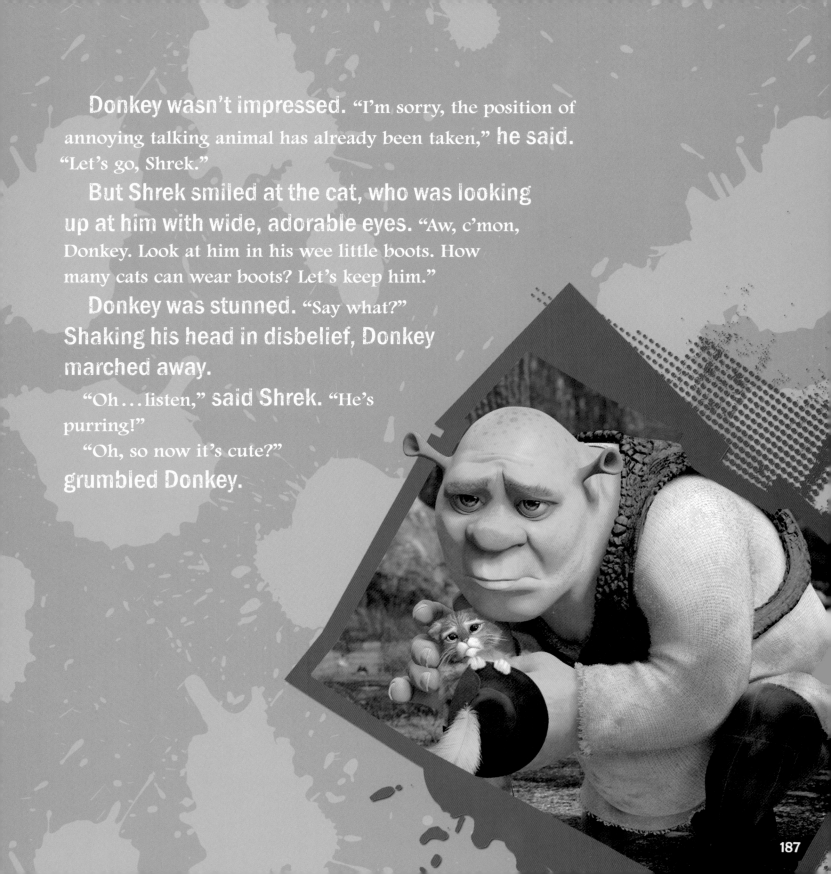

Shrek and Puss In Boots hurried to catch up with Donkey. Together they began their quest to visit Fairy Godmother and change Shrek's life...

...or maybe just to change Shrek.

DREAMWORKS

HOW TO TRAIN YOUR DRAGON

Befriending a Foe

It was a typical evening in the Viking village on the island of Berk. The kind of evening when everyone does their usual thing— eat supper, chat with friends...and battle dragons.

Battling dragons did not come
naturally to one scrawny teenager.
Hiccup was different from the other
rough-and-tumble Vikings. Instead of
fighting dragons with a sword and axe,
Hiccup designed complicated weapons
like a ball-and-rope-launching Mangler.

That night, as Deadly Nadders and Terrible Terrors filled the sky, Hiccup had a chance to try the Mangler.

Convinced he had brought down a legendary Night Fury, Hiccup confidently began dragon training the next day. When he took a beating from a Gronckle, though, he went on a walk to escape the jeers from the other teenagers.

In the woods, Hiccup noticed charred earth and destroyed trees. That could only mean one thing: a downed dragon. Hiccup gaped at the still body of a Night Fury—his invention, the Mangler, had worked!

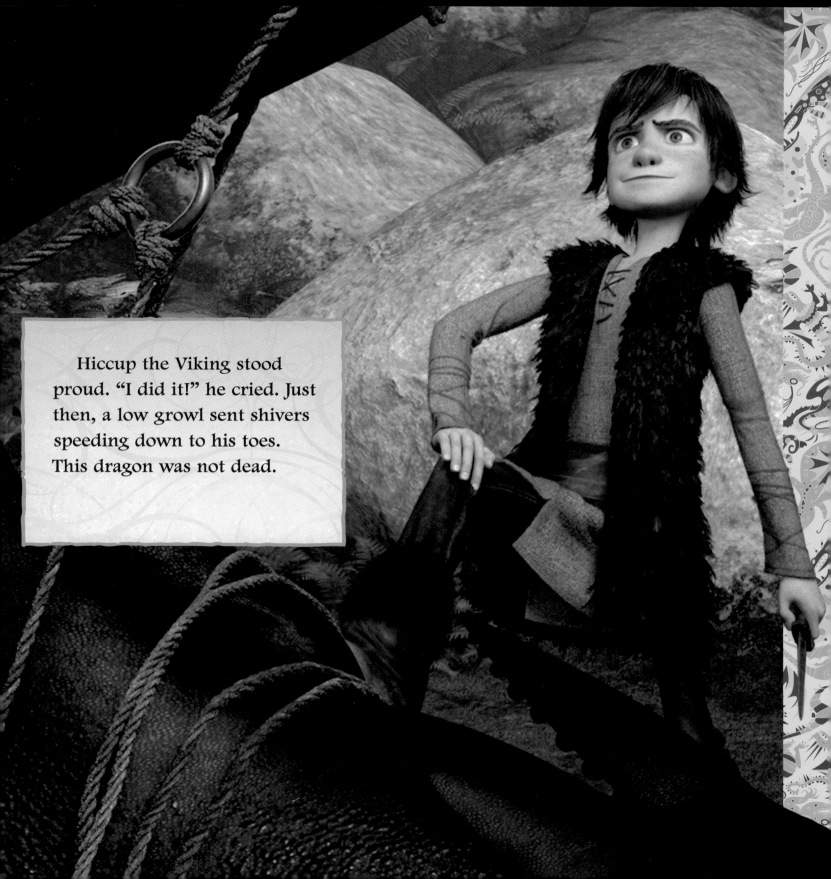

Hiccup the Viking stood proud. "I did it!" he cried. Just then, a low growl sent shivers speeding down to his toes. This dragon was not dead.

Hiccup scrambled for his dagger. Then he paused. Could he really kill this wounded creature?

Hiccup stared deeply into the dragon's eyes. "I'm going to kill you, dragon!" he declared. But he couldn't do it.

Hiccup looked at the dragon's wounds sympathetically. First he made sure no one was watching... then he cut the Mangler's ropes off the dragon.

THUMP! The Night Fury pounced on Hiccup, pinning him to the ground.

The powerful dragon stared deeply into Hiccup's eyes. Hiccup wondered if this was the last sight he'd ever see.

Then, to Hiccup's surprise, the Night Fury let him go and made his escape.

Later, Hiccup found the hurt dragon in a rocky cove. He could see the Night Fury's tail was broken and it couldn't fly. It couldn't catch any food, either. The mighty beast was fading and Hiccup had to help. He grabbed his sketchbook and began drafting plans for a new invention.

He worked in secret to build a new mechanical fin for the dragon.

When the fin was finished, Hiccup snuck through the village and into the woods to bring it to the Night Fury. He also brought a basket of fish for the dragon to eat.

The dragon warily approached the fish. Retractable teeth popped out of its gums as it grabbed the food and devoured it.

Hiccup placed a hand on the dragon's back as it ate. The creature seemed grateful for the meal Hiccup had provided.

As the dragon ate his fish, Hiccup struggled to get his invention onto the Night Fury's tail. Finally it was secure, and the dragon flew straight into the air with Hiccup holding on—until the fin fell off and they both crashed into the water.

After many more failed attempts, Hiccup perfected his mechanical tail invention and gained the trust of the beast.

At last, they were able to fly as a team! Hiccup gave small tugs on the dragon's tail fin. The wind whooshed, the waves crashed, and the new friends soared high over their ancient island.

A dragon and a Viking, friends? No one on the island of Berk had ever imagined the idea. Hiccup would never have believed it himself.

The Furious Five

There was trouble at Chogun prison, where the only prisoner was the evil snow leopard Tai Lung. Long ago, the former kung fu master had tried to steal the Dragon Scroll—and its secret to unlimited power—for himself.

A single goose feather was all Tai Lung needed to pick the lock on his shackles. He used his awesome kung fu skills to overpower the guards and escape, leaving the prison in ruins.

Tai Lung headed straight for the Valley of Peace.

News of the breakout quickly reached the Valley of Peace. Each of the Furious Five kung fu masters hoped to become the chosen Dragon Warrior who would protect the Valley from Tai Lung.

The local villagers crowded into the Jade Palace arena as the five masters began to compete.

Monkey, Mantis, and Viper dazzled the crowd with kung fu skills.

Then Crane dodged rockets fired from a wooden dragon. Finally, Tigress leaped into the ring to face the Iron Ox. The crowd gasped as she executed her legendary split kick.

"I sense the Dragon Warrior is among us," announced Master Oogway.

The crowed hushed. The Five waited for Oogway's choice. Each wanted to be the new hero and learn the secret of the Dragon Scroll.

Then, suddenly... *THUD!* As if he had been dropped from the sky, a giant panda named Po crash-landed right in front of them!

"Uh...sorry," he said.

But this was no accident. This was destiny!
"The universe has brought us the Dragon
Warrior," declared Master Oogway, pointing.
The Five were confused.

"Master, are you pointing at . . . me?" Tigress asked.

"No, him," replied Master Oogway.

"Me?" asked the confused panda.

"Yes, you!" exclaimed the wise tortoise.

Po was the Dragon Warrior? Impossible!
The Dragon Warrior was supposed to be the most
powerful warrior ever. How could a flabby panda
possibly protect the Valley of Peace?

Later, Po joined the Furious Five in their training hall. Mantis flew through the air, dodging spiked clubs. Viper coiled her body to spring away from shooting flames.

Monkey leaped through
hoops covered in sharp claws
while Tigress and Crane sparred
on the rim of a wobbling jade bowl.

As the new Dragon Warrior, Po now had to face the same harsh obstacle course. Everyone watched as Po approached the gauntlet and...*BAM!* The panda was sucked in and spit back out in a matter of minutes, bruised and scorched.

222

"Feeling a little nauseous," Po said.
The Furious Five shook their heads. They
knew Po would be bad. But not *this* bad!

"We've waited a thousand years for the Dragon Warrior," complained Tigress. "One would think Master Oogway would choose someone who actually knew kung fu."

Monkey agreed. But Mantis wasn't so sure. Maybe there was more to Po than they realized. He knew better than anyone that heroes come in all shapes and sizes.

The Five knew that Tai Lung was coming. Tigress didn't believe Po could protect the Valley.

"This is what we've been trained for," she declared.

The others agreed. They would battle Tai Lung themselves.

226

The brave warriors left at night and raced over the village rooftops until its peaceful borders were far behind.

The Furious Five reached a rope bridge that
stretched across a deep gorge. Suddenly, on the far
side of the bridge, they saw him—Tai Lung!
  Tigress rocketed across the bridge to attack. The
two cats battled in a blur of fists and fur.

228

Monkey leaped into action, too. He kicked Tai Lung right in the chest while Viper lashed at the vicious leopard with her tail.

But Tai Lung was too strong. He defeated the Furious Five with his paralyzing nerve attack!

"I thought we could stop him," said Tigress as the battered warriors arrived home.

"He's too strong. Too fast!" added Monkey. The Furious Five finally had to face the truth... none of them could beat Tai Lung. Not one of them was the Dragon Warrior.

They all looked at Po. He had been training hard while they were gone. Seeing him now, the Furious Five realized that Po had hidden talents. They felt bad about unfairly judging the big panda.

The Five urged Po to accept the Dragon Scroll as the new Dragon Warrior.

Whatever secret Po found in the scroll, the Furious Five would be right there to help him fight Tai Lung. And they now believed that he could win.

The sun was shining at the New York Zoo. It was a perfect day for Maurice to relax. And, boy, did he need a break from King Julien. "Making my ice-cream, mm-hmm!" Maurice sang happily. He bent down to grab a cherry for his ice-cream sundae. But when he popped back up, his sundae was gone. King Julien had eaten it! "Less sprinkles next time," the king said.

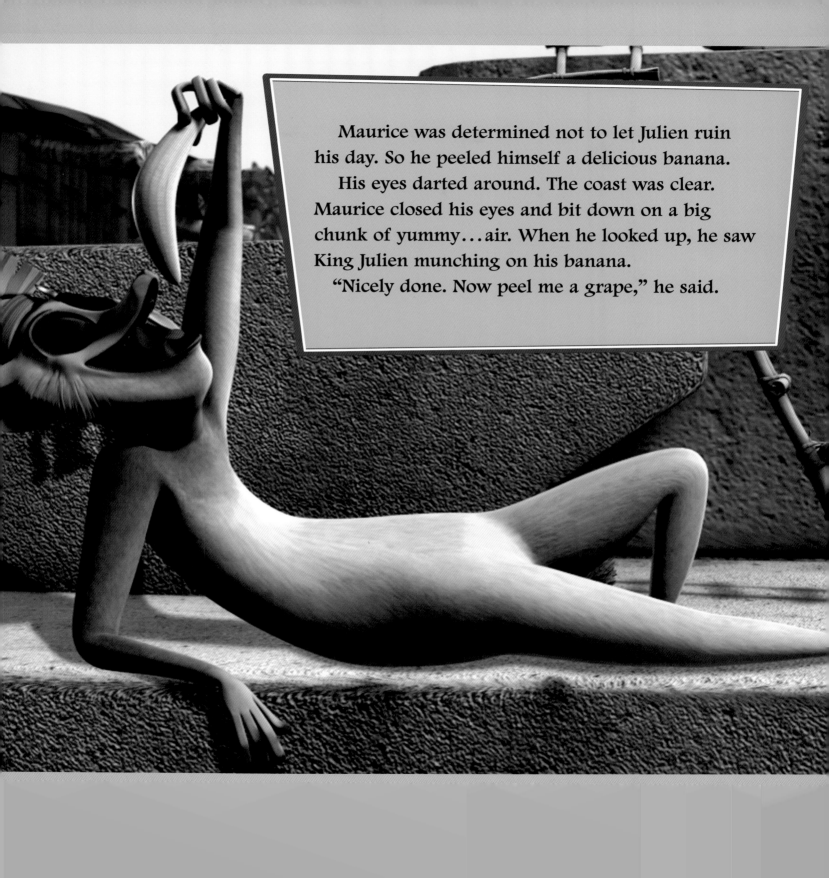

Maurice was determined not to let Julien ruin his day. So he peeled himself a delicious banana. His eyes darted around. The coast was clear. Maurice closed his eyes and bit down on a big chunk of yummy…air. When he looked up, he saw King Julien munching on his banana.

"Nicely done. Now peel me a grape," he said.

Nearby, the penguins kicked back in the sun with some frozen drinks.

"Private, these sardine smoothies are top-notch. What's your secret?" asked Skipper.

"Love, sir. I made them with love," said Private, proud of his recipe. This alarmed Skipper. He slapped the drinks out of everyone's wings.

"No more love in the smoothies!" he barked. "We've got to stay sharp."

Rico burped, possibly in agreement. It was hard to tell.

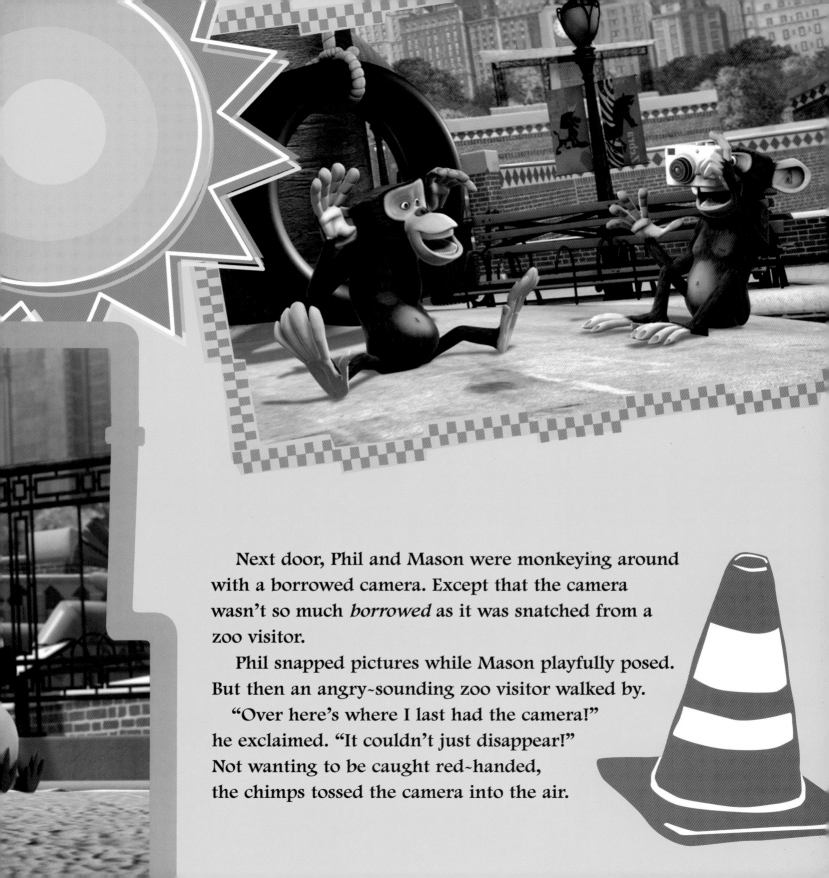

Next door, Phil and Mason were monkeying around with a borrowed camera. Except that the camera wasn't so much *borrowed* as it was snatched from a zoo visitor.

Phil snapped pictures while Mason playfully posed. But then an angry-sounding zoo visitor walked by.

"Over here's where I last had the camera!" he exclaimed. "It couldn't just disappear!" Not wanting to be caught red-handed, the chimps tossed the camera into the air.

The camera flew through the air, landing in Maurice's hands. King Julien snatched the camera from Maurice. But Maurice was tired of Julien's sticky fingers.

"Gimme!" demanded King Julien, tugging at the camera. "What part of *gim* or *me* did you not understand?"

"I understood the *me* part. Like this was caught by *me*, for *me*!" Maurice yelled, pulling the camera with all his might.

During their fierce tug~of~war, King Julien accidentally pressed a button on the camera. A flash of blinding light went off. Maurice and the king tumbled in opposite directions. The camera landed with a thud.

The king sat up, feeling dazed. Maurice was nowhere to be seen.

"Maurice?" he called. "Where are you and your booty which is quite large and is usually easy to see?"

Then Mort picked up the camera. An image of Maurice was on the screen.

"He's trapped!" Mort screamed.

"Uh...yes. That is what happens when you question the king's power!" King Julien said, thinking Maurice was stuck inside the camera.

Julien stared at the camera, waiting for Maurice to say something.

"Oh," he said. "You are giving to me the 'silent treatment.' I, too, can give you *the treatment*!"

The penguins walked by, witnessing Julien's fury. "Speaking to a camera. This is not normal," stated Skipper.

"Maurice questioned my kingly authority, so now he's trapped in this magic thingy, which the sky spirits sent me, the king," King Julien explained.

Skipper rolled his eyes. There was no way to make the king believe the camera wasn't magical. "All right, boys. Let's leave the madman to his madness," he said.

241

Then Skipper felt a tiny tug on his wing. It was Mort, looking worried.
"Spit it out, sad eyes," Skipper said.

"The king's giving Maurice *the treatment*," Mort whispered. "He's going to
leave him in the magic box. You have to help get him out. Pleeeeeease!" Then he
batted his eyelashes to look extra cute. This had no effect on Skipper.

Skipper patted Mort on the head. Clearly his little mammal brain didn't understand. "That is a camera, and your little pal is not in it," Skipper told him.

Then Private piped in. "But Skipper, where is he?"

He had a point. Skipper decided to lead an investigation to find the missing lemur. "Let's crack this mystery wide open," Skipper said. "We're looking for anything that might be a clue."

Armed with a magnifying glass, Rico began to inspect his surroundings. First he found a banana peel, which he ate right away.

"Hey, mister, that's evidence," scolded Skipper. Then he peered through Rico's magnifying glass. There were lemur tracks leading off the edge of the platform!

Then Skipper took a closer look. "My guess is he stumbled backwards. But why?" he said.

Private had a theory. "Maybe the camera's flash blinded him?" he offered.

"Sounds a little preposterous, Private," said Skipper. "But just in case...Kowalski, run a temporarily blinded, portly lemur scenario."

Kowalski brought Rico to the edge of the platform where Maurice's footprints ended. There was only one way to find out what had happened to the lemur.

"Stand right here, Rico," Kowalski said. Then, suddenly, Kowalski pushed him off the ledge. Rico fell down, landing on the king's blow-up bouncy toy. He sprang back into the air and over the wall, landing inside a trash can!

The penguins zipped over to the trash can. Skipper spied a trash collector throwing garbage into a rolling dumpster.

"I know exactly what happened," assured Skipper. "Into the can, men."

Moments later, the penguins were inside the trash can. Then, just like Skipper thought, the trash collector tossed them inside the dumpster.

Later that night, the penguins reached their destination: the dump.

Skipper sprung out of the trash heap like a jack-in-the-box.

"Kowalski, coordinates!" he barked.

"New Jersey," Kowalski answered, spotting a license plate in the trash around him.

Skipper happily inhaled a whiff of garbage. "All right, listen up," he said. "We are going to search this dump high and low."

Then Private shouted out, "Skipper, over here!" The penguins waddled over to Private, who had already found Maurice.

"What are you doing here?" Maurice asked.

"We're here to rescue you," said Private.

Maurice shook his head. "No way. No how," said Maurice. "I have had it with Julien. He's been a royal pain in my tail for too long."

After some convincing, the penguins finally talked Maurice into going home with them. He couldn't live in a dump forever! So the penguins began to race along the open road, dodging cars on the trek back to the zoo.

"This is insane! You are insane!" Maurice yelled, trying to keep up.

The group soon approached a highway tollbooth. The penguins and Maurice needed to pay to pass through.

"Rico!" Skipper ordered.

Rico knew just what to do. On command, he coughed up the correct amount of coins so they could pass through the gate.

251

Then the group began walking along some empty train tracks. Maurice was lagging behind.

"Gotta...rest..." he gasped, trying to catch his breath.

"No dice," said Skipper. "We have to be back at the zoo by oh~nine~hundred hours."

"Which does not give us much time," added Kowalski.

"There's no way I can go faster!" said Maurice.

Skipper gave Maurice a knowing pat on the back. "The ol' D train might change your tune," he said.

"The what?" asked Maurice. But instead of answering him, the penguins took a running start and slid down the side rails. Maurice was left clueless until, seconds later, a bright light began to shine on the lemur. A horn wailed. A train was coming!

"Aaaaah!" screamed Maurice, running as fast as he could.

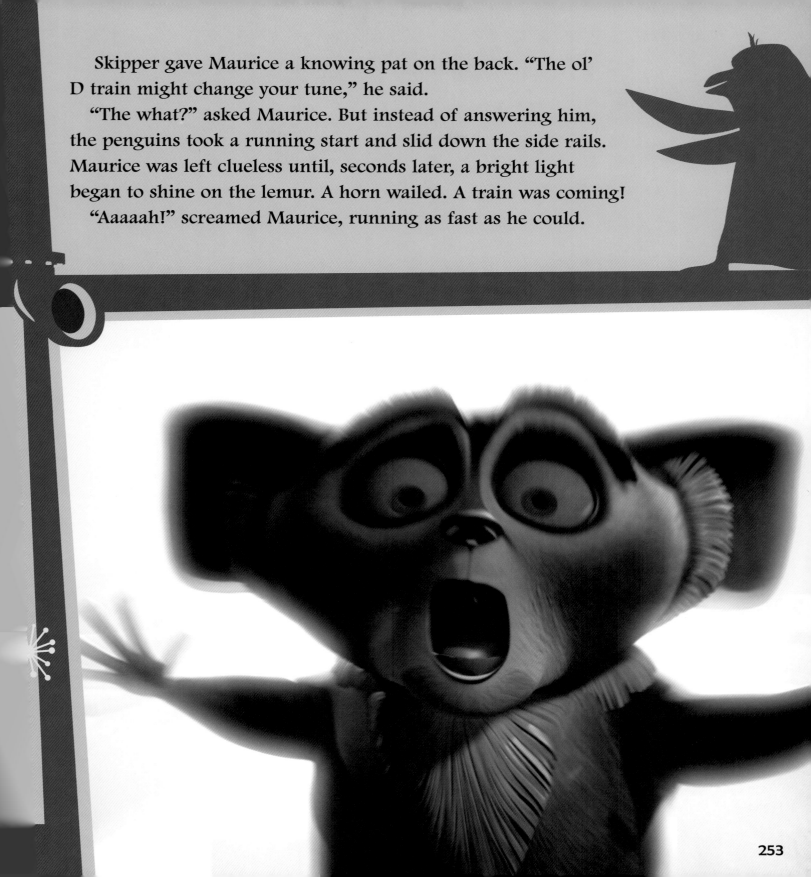

Back at the zoo, King Julien was staring at Maurice's picture.

"Stop looking at me like that!" he told the camera. "I am shutting up now because you are still getting the *shhh* treatment."

But deep down, the king missed his friend. He hugged the camera tightly.

"I can't take it anymore. You win!" he cried. "I will give anything to get my big-bootied buddy back!"

Then King Julien had a brilliant idea. He could smash the camera with a heavy rock tied to a vine. "Now we break poor Maurice out of his magical prison!" Julien announced.

Mort placed the camera underneath the rock. "A little to the left," King Julien told Mort.

Mort scratched his head. "My left or your left?" he asked innocently.

"Mine, of course!" King Julien said. "I am king. The lefts are all mine!"

Meanwhile, the penguins and Maurice were almost home. On the streets of New York City, Skipper saw a bus headed toward the zoo. The penguins tossed Maurice inside. After a short ride, Maurice stumbled down the bus steps, exhausted from the hectic journey.

"All right, boys," announced Skipper. "Commence Operation Shoot the Moon!"

The penguins put together a makeshift catapult. They wanted to fling Maurice over the zoo wall to get him back home.

Private saddled himself into the catapult for a test run. Rico pulled back on the catapult and let go. Private arced through the air and...*SPLAT*! He smashed into the brick wall.

"Ooof!" he yelled, sliding down the wall.

Kowalski quickly made some adjustments to the catapult. Then Skipper called Maurice over. "Lemur! You're up!" he said, slapping Maurice cheerfully on the back.

Maurice stepped backward, his whole body quaking with fear. "I can't take it anymore! You penguins are psychotic!" he yelled.

But Kowalski grabbed Maurice and plunked him down in the launch seat. Seconds later, Maurice was slicing through the air.

"Aaaaaah!" he screamed.

At the lemur habitat, King Julien was still ordering Mort to move the camera around so he could smash it to bits.

"Mort, a little more to the left," the king said.

Finally, Julien was satisfied with the camera's position. He released the vine and dropped the big rock onto the camera, and... *BAM!* King Julien dropped the rock directly on top of Mort.

"Eeeee!" yelled a squashed Mort.

King Julien didn't even notice that Mort was being squished. He rushed toward the camera and knelt down to talk to it. "Maurice!" he cried out. "I want you back! Great sky spirits, hear my plea!"

Just then, Maurice fell from the sky and landed on the camera's flash button.

FLASH! The blinding light sent King Julien reeling backward. He sat there for a second, stunned at the appearance of Maurice, who was lying on top of the camera. "Maurice!" King Julien exclaimed.

The king scooped up his pal in a big upside-down hug. "I am so glad you are back!" King Julien exclaimed.

Maurice knew one thing for sure: Tolerating King Julien might be a big pain in his booty, but it was far better than spending one more terrifying second with those crazy penguins.

"It's good to see you, too," Maurice said, meaning every word.

In the middle of their special moment,
Skipper waddled over to the king and Maurice.
"Mission accomplished," Skipper said proudly.
The king shook his head in disbelief. "Oh, as if
you had anything to do with it. The sky
spirits released Maurice!" Then King Julien
looked up, throwing his hands in the air. "You
rock, sky spirits!" he shouted.

Skipper arched an eyebrow. "Why don't you tell the king what really happened, rescued mammal?" he said to Maurice.

But after his time spent with the penguins, Maurice knew exactly how to answer Skipper. He stuck out his chest and proudly announced, "Rule number one: Do not question the king!"

The PENGUINS of MADAGASCAR

DREAMWORKS

TWO FEET HIGH and RISING

Maurice was tired from filling up balloons all day. He was making King Julien's chair into a Super Comfy Pamper Time Floaty Throne. Then King Julien could relax in style while sailing high above his royal subjects at the zoo.

Finally, King Julien allowed Maurice to take a break to do another job. His Gorgeousness needed grooming. "Let's get this pampering over with," Maurice muttered.

Meanwhile, little Mort sat in a corner. He longed to be the one brushing King Julien's royal fur. Mort worshipped King Julien from his crown down to his furry feet—especially those handsome toes!

267

When Maurice's brush reached the fabulous feet, the king shoved him away. "Ah, ah, ah!" he said. "There is only one set of hands that is fitting to be touching the royal feet..."

Mort's eyes grew bigger than ever. Could he dare to hope for such an honor?

"...and that," Julien concluded, "is the hands of the king himself!"

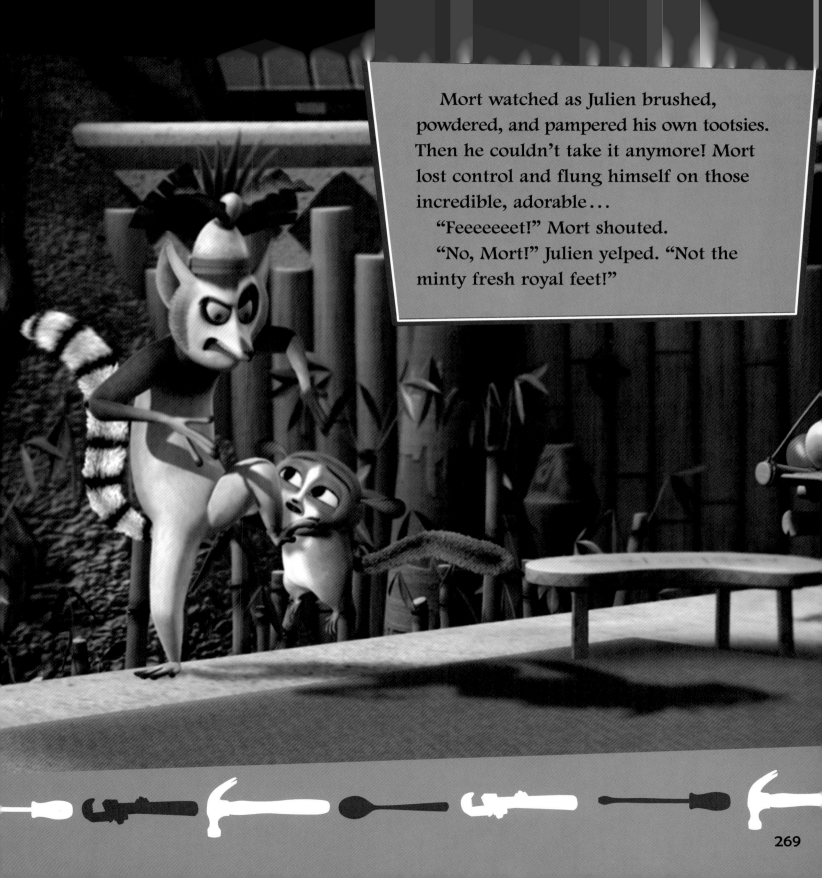

Mort watched as Julien brushed, powdered, and pampered his own tootsies. Then he couldn't take it anymore! Mort lost control and flung himself on those incredible, adorable...

"Feeeeeet!" Mort shouted.

"No, Mort!" Julien yelped. "Not the minty fresh royal feet!"

King Julien managed to kick Mort free of his feet. But he had had enough of this nonsense. Later that day, King Julien assembled all of the animals.

"From now on," he announced, "anyone who dares to be touching my beautiful feets shall be banished from my kingdom. Forever!"

Then King Julien presented his no-foot-touching sign. "I drew that," he boasted.

Everyone thought the lemur had lost his mind. Especially the penguins.

"What kind of sickie would want to touch his feet, anyway?" Marlene the otter remarked.

Meanwhile, little Mort stared at King Julien's feet and sighed from the bottom of his soul. How could he possibly resist the lure of the royal lemur's furry, fantastic feet?

That night, Mort was too upset to sleep. Even in his dreams, Mort yearned for the royal feet. Afraid that he could not control himself, Mort chained himself to a tree. But not even chains could keep Mort from those toes! He broke free, attracted like a magnet to King Julien's tootsies.

"What in the feets are you doings?!" King Julien screamed. "You are hereby banished from my kingdom...FOREVER!"

273

Mort slouched away from the lemur habitat, feeling lower than the pavement. Where could he go? What would he do? Whose feet would he love?

Then Marlene saw the lonely looking lemur. "Sorry to hear about the whole foot-banishing thing," she said. "If there's anything I can do…"

But before she could finish her sentence, Mort leaped into Marlene's arms. "Help me? Cure me? Fix me? Save me?" he gushed.

"I'm an otter, not a miracle worker," Marlene replied. But she had an idea.

Marlene took Mort to Penguin Headquarters. She was sure the penguins could help him get over his foot obsession.

But Skipper refused. "Negative, Marlene. We are not accepting new recruits. Besides, Mort is . . ."

"He's not that bad!" Marlene fibbed. But Skipper knew better. The truth was smeared all over the floor: Mort had drawn green footprints all over it!

"Okay, he's bad," Marlene admitted. "But that's why he needs you! You're a role model! A natural leader!"

Skipper fell for her flattery...and for Mort's big, begging eyes.

"Son, I'm gonna mold you in my hand like a lump of wet clay," Skipper announced.

"Yippee!" said Mort. "I like wet clay!"

277

Skipper and the other penguins took the little lemur under their flippers. They used big cardboard feet to train Mort out of his foot-hugging habit. If Mort touched a cardboard foot, he got a tiny electric shock!

After a few dozen shocking hugs, even Mort's itty-bitty brain finally began to connect *foot* with *bad*.

Next, Private tried helping Mort in a gentler way. "Say it with me," Private said. "They're just feet, not love."

Thanks to lots of encouragement from the penguins, Mort learned to say, "They're just feet, not love."

Mort even learned to run between all the giant cardboard feet, shouting, "No! No hug for you! Or you!"

But sometimes, Mort just couldn't help himself. One cardboard foot looked so cute, the loving little lemur said, "Okay, one hug!" Then, as soon as he did... "OW!"

To prevent this from happening again, the penguins tried extreme measures. They put on gas masks and borrowed Alice the zookeeper's super-stinky boot. Then the penguins shoved Mort's face right into it!

Stunned by the stench, Mort stumbled away in a daze. "King Julien's...feet...bad," he mumbled.

Finally, Mort was cured. The penguins took off their masks and gave Mort a gold medal.

"The boy is 100 percent lemur foot–phobic," Kowalski told Marlene.

"He won't even be touching his own toes," Skipper added.

Marlene wasn't sure if that was such a good thing. But before she could say so, a high shriek from the sky above shocked them all!

Private pointed toward the sky. "Skipper, look!" he exclaimed.
Skipper needed a closer look. "Rico!" he shouted.
Rico instantly coughed up just what his leader needed: a pair of binoculars made from plastic cups.

Through the binoculars, the penguins saw King Julien rising high above the zoo in his Super Comfy Pamper Time Floaty Throne. Maurice must have finally managed to tie more balloons to it—but it looked like he had added too many!

"Help! I am in need of helpings!" King Julien cried as he drifted toward the clock tower.

"Hot dog! Ringtail's in trouble!" Skipper exclaimed. "Suit up, men." Then he turned to Mort and added, "You too."

In minutes, they made a hang glider out of things they found around the zoo.

"Operation Luft Balloons is a go," said Skipper as the penguins flew toward King Julien. Meanwhile, Mort ran for the clock tower.

285

To everyone's alarm, the King's Floaty Throne floated right into the clock! As King Julien thrashed in mindless panic, balloon strings and clock hands became hopelessly tangled.

"Cheese and crackers, man!" Skipper shouted. "Struggling will just make it worse!"

"Eh?! I cannot hear you over my frantic and panicked strugglings!" the king shouted.
  Suddenly, the lounge chair crashed to the pavement below. King Julien was left
dangling in the air, held only by a few balloon strings. The remaining balloons were
beginning to burst.
  The penguins reached for the terrified lemur…

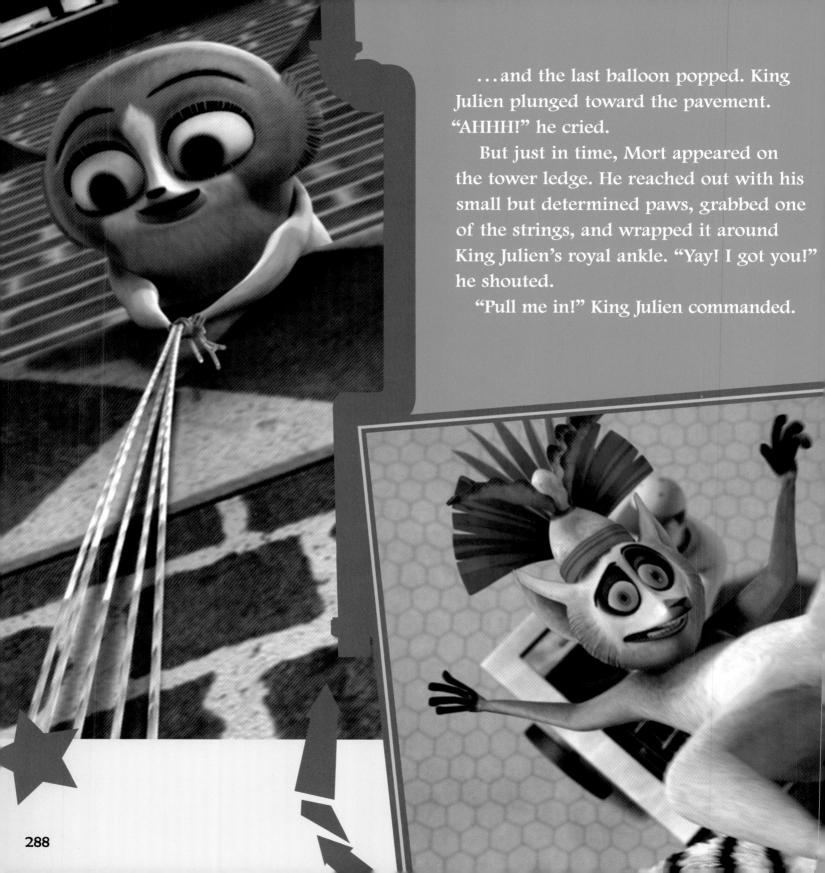

...and the last balloon popped. King Julien plunged toward the pavement. "AHHH!" he cried.

But just in time, Mort appeared on the tower ledge. He reached out with his small but determined paws, grabbed one of the strings, and wrapped it around King Julien's royal ankle. "Yay! I got you!" he shouted.

"Pull me in!" King Julien commanded.

Mort wanted to obey his beloved king. But he had a problem. As Mort pulled the strings up, the royal feet came closer and closer. Little Mort did not know much. But he had learned one thing recently: "King Julien's feet...bad!" he said.

Julien saw the strings starting to fray. "What?! No! Feet good! Please! Touch my feet! Grab them!" he pleaded. Mort felt torn between his heart and his training. "Hold my feet! Love them!" Julien begged.

Just as the string snapped and Julien started to fall, the smallest lemur did a very big thing. He overcame his newfound fear of feet—and saved the king by grabbing his foot!

"Well, I'll be knitted and darned," said Skipper. "He did it. The freaky foot lover did it."

When he was safely on the ground, King Julien once again called all of the zoo animals together. "Attentions, peoples," he announced. "I am hereby decreeing that my new 'no feet touching' decree is a decree I am removing forever!"

But the animals weren't satisfied. This was not what they had come to hear.
King Julien knew what he had to say. "Okay, fine. I also officially thank Mort
for saving me, welcome him back to the kingdom, blah, blah, blah..."
Mort could not contain his joy. "I'm home!" he shouted.

Mort wanted to run straight for the royal feet. How he had missed them! But would the king really let him touch his perfect kingly toes? There was only one way to find out.

"No! Not the feet!" King Julien shouted.
But Mort would not be denied.
"Fine," King Julien sighed. "I shall be permitting one hug.
How bad could one hug be?"

Mort hugged the king's funny feet with all his might. Then, to Julien's dismay, Mort burst into song. "A singing hug?!" Julien shrieked. "Ah! It's bad!"

But Mort wasn't listening.
He just kept hugging and singing. The little
lemur was thrilled to finally be back where
he belonged—with his favorite pair of feet!

The
end